ZERO HOUR

A PREQUEL TO ZERO TOLERANCE

AUTUMN JONES LAKE

ZERO HOUR (Lost Kings MC #11.5)
A prequel to Zero Tolerance
DIGITAL ISBN#: 978-1-943950-35-5
PRINT ISBN #: 978-1-943950-97-3

Cover Model: Justin Cox
Photographer: Wander Aguiar
Cover Designed by: Autumn Jones Lake

The night we met, I only tagged along to support my best friend. Then I saw Lilly. There's no harm in picking up a girl for myself, right?

A few hours with her underneath me. No longer than a night. That's all I ever need with a woman. I'm the Vice President of the Lost Kings MC. There's no shortage of women waiting to warm my bed.

But one night isn't enough. I can't get her out of my head, even though she makes it clear she's not available. Suddenly, I find myself seeking Lilly out on holidays and special occasions, using any excuse to be near her.

That's when I realize she's the only one I want to spend all my nights with.

Now if I can convince her what we have amounts to more than a few lust-filled hours.

I'm not sure how it all got so twisted, but this is how it all begins...

NOTE FROM AUTUMN

DEAR READER,

Thank you so much for purchasing Zero Hour!

Allow me to give you some background on how this collection came to be. The first story, *Infatuated* appeared in an anthology that was only available for a short time back in 2015 and I've always meant to make it available to my readers again. With the release of Z's first full-length book, Zero Tolerance (Lost Kings MC #12), I thought it would be the perfect time to bring *Infatuated* back! And what better way to introduce Z and Lilly to new readers? But *Infatuated* was kind of short (about 5,000 words) so I thought, hey, why not add the other two short stories about Z and Lilly and even add two new pieces!

And that's how Zero Hour was born!

If you're new to the Lost Kings MC series, welcome! This is a great place to start!

If you've already been inducted into the Lost Kings MC family, welcome back! I know you've been waiting a LONG time for Z's story and I love you so much for your faith in me and your patience with me! Thank you so much!

xo,

Autumn

INFATUATED

Infatuated is a short story that was originally included in the PINK: Hot 'n Sexy for a Cure Anthology.

Zero

My president is finally gonna make this happen.

President, as in the president of my motorcycle club and one of my best friends. Known Rock since I was a teenager. Love him like a brother. There aren't many things I won't do for him.

Including eating dinner at an obnoxious, yuppie hangout while we wait for the woman he's had a hard-on for about two years now to show up.

Whatever. I'm along for the ride to make sure my brother doesn't beat the shit out of someone before Hope gets here. He's *that* wound up over the pretty lawyer.

While we're finishing our food, Rock nods to the front door. "That's Sophie," he says, indicating a thin, dark-haired woman. She glances up and winks at us.

Now I understand how he got talked into this whole thing. "Hot."

Rock glares at me and I laugh. Christ, his girl better show up, or he's gonna be one grumpy fucker.

I'm not laughing two seconds later when Sophie's friend follows her in. Now, *she's* a knock-out.

"Who's the one with the big tits?"

Another glare from him. "Don't know."

I called her that to make him laugh, when really it's her big, expressive eyes and long, almost black hair that grabs my attention.

It's another half hour before Rock's girl shows up. He's so tense I'm surprised he doesn't explode at the sight of her. Yet, he doesn't make his move right away.

Time to poke the lion. "Your girl's here now."

"Yeah, she's here," he answers without looking at me.

"Gonna go talk to her, or sit there like a stump all night drooling over her tight ass?"

"Not yet." He turns his death glare on me. "And keep your eyes off her ass."

I shrug and try not to laugh again.

The plan is for Sophie to get Hope drunk so Rock can swoop in and offer her a ride home.

My plan is to get Big Tits alone. Maybe even find out her name. Definitely find out what color her eyes are and if her tits are real or not.

The girls go through a round of drinks. After a while, they're loud enough to hear all the way up here.

"Let's go." Rock stands and motions me down the stairs. 'Bout fuckin' time. People hurry to get out of our way. I doubt this bar sees many bikers. Certainly none with the ferocious face Rock's wearing.

Smooth as a motherfucker, Rock slides in behind her. She reaches out to him and all his smooth vanishes. He can't even answer the simple question she asks. I consider letting him flounder but finally rescue my brother.

"Just in the area and got hungry. How you doin', Hope?"

I don't think I've actually ever officially met her, but she's too drunk to question me. Hasn't let go of Rock's hand yet, either.

"Who are your friends, Hope?" Big Tits asks after Hope and Rock finish eye-fucking each other some more.

Across the table, Sophie giggles and bumps her shoulder into Big Tits.

Hope shakes her head and turns toward her friends. "Rock, you've met Sophie, this is Lilly, Mara, and Ross is over at the bar. Guys, this is a former client of mine, Rock, and—"

"Z," I offer with a smile aimed at Big Tits...Lilly. *Lilly.* Rolls right off my tongue. I am *definitely* fucking her.

While they discuss who's driving where, I catch Lilly's eye. "Where you headed, sugar?"

Jesus Christ. When she tilts her head in my direction and focuses her big brown eyes my way, I forget to breathe. Her perfect pouty pink lips curve into a seductive smile. "You planning to drive me all the way up to Lake George?" she asks in a throaty voice. *Hell yes.* I'll drive her to the Mexican border and back if she'll say my name in her phone-sex-operator purr all night.

"I'll take the drive," I answer a little too fast.

After Rock takes Hope home, I focus all my charms on Lilly.

One way or another, I want her under me tonight.

Lilly

It seems like Sophie's plan to get Hope and Rock together is going to work out well for me too. Holy fuck, I've never seen a hotter guy than...Z. He hasn't been willing to disclose his real name yet.

Doesn't matter, he can give me a ride anywhere he wants. Preferably on that big, sexy body of his. What he has underneath his hooded sweatshirt and leather vest looks promising.

All his good looks and charm probably mean he's a lousy lay. In my experience, most guys who spend that much time keeping themselves in shape are either compensating for tiny dicks and lousy skills or assume women are so eager to jump into bed with them, they don't have to make an effort.

My stomach flips when we step outside and I run my gaze over his bike. Pressing myself up against him for the forty-five-minute drive while that big machine rumbles underneath us—I'm in trouble. Z glances at me and I swear there's concern darkening his perfect features. "You're gonna be chilly, Lilly," he says. We stare at each other, then laugh at the rhyme.

My gaze travels over his body. "You'll make it worth it, right?"

"Hell yeah." One corner of his mouth lifts in a sexy smirk. Then he shrugs out of his leather vest, pulls off his hooded sweatshirt and hands it over. I raise an eyebrow at his outstretched arm. "Now you'll be cold."

"Snuggle up tight against me."

Yeah, like that's a hardship.

Thinking of the things I want him to do to me when we get to my house keeps me warm on the drive up the Northway.

"You wanna get a drink?" Z shouts over the roar of the bike. He slows to take the ramp that will lead us into the village. Since it's early spring, the resort town doesn't have many shops or eateries open.

"Sure!" I shout back. He seems to know the area well because he easily rides through town, looping through the park and finally glides right into an open spot in front of one of the year-round townie bars.

Mikey's Pub still has a fair number of people filling the

tiny space this late at night. We grab a quiet table in the back. After placing drink orders, Z moves his chair next to mine. Close enough for our elbows and thighs to touch.

"So, Lilly, friend of Hope, what do you do?"

I hate answering this question. Most guys look at my big tits, long legs, and pretty face and assume I'm stupid. This guy is purely sex, so I don't give a fuck about impressing him. I doubt he'll understand what my job is even if I explain it using construction paper and crayons.

Fuck it. "I'm a policy analyst for the legislature."

His face registers surprise…and interest? Okay, that's new.

"What's that like?" he asks.

I shrug. "Boring most days. People ask for my opinion all the time, but no one wants to actually implement the changes I suggest. New York is tough because it's such a politically diverse state." I'm about to go off on a tangent, so I stop myself. That's not what tonight is about, right?

"Yeah, I always thought we should just cut everything below Westchester County off and let them fend for themselves."

"Typical Upstate opinion. A lot of money flows from NYC though."

His lips twist in a wry grin. "Lotta bullshit too."

"What do you do?"

He points to his vice president patch.

"That's it? VP of a Motorcycle Club?" I didn't mean to sound so dismissive.

His eyes narrow, but there's a glimmer of amusement there so I don't think he minds.

"It keeps me busy. The MC owns Crystal Ball. Right now, I manage it with one of the other guys."

I burst out laughing. "I know CB well. I used to dance at Club Salvatore before you guys had it shut down."

He doesn't bother denying that his club was responsible for the shutdown. "No shit?"

Our waitress drops off our drinks and we both remain silent until she leaves.

"No shit. That's how I paid for undergrad and my master's degree."

"I'm impressed. Lot of girls say they're just dancing until they finish school. Few ever leave the life."

"Yeah, well, tits are only perky for so long. No one wants to see old and wrinkly twirling around the pole."

His sensual mouth twists into a grin. "Babe, I can't imagine there is anything old and wrinkly on that body."

"Not yet. I'm just saying, I saw plenty of girls like you're talking about. Looks don't last forever. I wanted something more secure so I made sure I finished school."

"Good plan. What else do you do?"

"Are we really doing this? I thought the appeal of a one-night stand was cutting out the small talk."

"Whoa." He places his hand over his heart. "What an assumption. I'm just offering a pretty girl a ride home."

"Oh, sorry, I didn't realize you expected me to play hard to get. Continue." I'm intrigued. Z has this peculiar charm that gets my blood simmering. I expected a filthy, dirty, sex god biker, but instead, he's playful and charming.

"No, babe, I like direct. That totally works for me."

"So, we *are* going to fuck?" I blurt out. What's wrong with me tonight? Normally, I enjoy the coy chase and seduction games. But this guy has my panties so soaked I'm afraid to stand up.

"Absolutely." His warm hand curls around mine, picking it up so he can brush his lips over the back. My skin tingles everywhere he touches. His other hand lands on my leg under the table, slowly trailing under my dress, up my thigh. My legs part and his fingers brush against the satin crotch of my underwear. His eyes widen when he feels how wet they are. His sexy lips press against my ear. "Let's fuck here. I'll meet you in the bathroom."

My palm wraps around his bicep, a handful of granite muscle. Christ, that's hot. I've missed muscle and men who actually care about their appearance more than their fat wallets.

"You can't be serious," I manage to protest.

"Like fuck I'm not." His finger strokes a little harder against my satin-covered pussy lips. "You're wet and ready. I'm hard as a fucking hammer. Let's go."

Wow. I'm in serious trouble because I can't stop myself from imagining him fucking me up against the wall in the bathroom. Him pushing my dress up around my hips while ripping my panties off. Our sweaty bodies sliding against the ancient wood paneling. Pure, furious, raw fucking.

I can't believe I'm actually considering it.

Then my practical side kicks in. There's the danger of getting caught and never being able to show my face in Mikey's Pub again.

Even worse, the wrong person could catch us, the cops are called and my career swirls down the toilet.

"No." *What now? Did I just turn this hotter than sin man down?*

Yes. Yes, I did and I have a completely a logical reason.

I can't remember what that reason is with his finger gently stroking over my clit. *Fuck.*

He pulls away. "No?"

Thank God he stopped. Now I can think.

"No. No sweaty, quick fuck." I give his bicep a squeeze. "I want to see you in all your naked glory. I have a feeling there's one spectacular body under there."

Am I nuts or did his cheeks turn a tad pink?

"Yeah, okay. Ditto. Where?"

"My place."

He quirks an eyebrow. "You're okay bringing the biker thug home with you?"

What an odd question.

"Well, yeah. You're not going to mug me, are you?"

His face breaks into a grin, and I realize he's got these amazing dimples. A biker with dimples. He'll probably shoot me if I tell him how cute he is.

"No. But you were right. No quick fuck." Another

smile. Another peek at his dimples. Unreal. A couple seconds after shutting him down and he's amused.

"Is that right?" My voice barely rises above the thumping in my chest.

He leans in closer, warm lips brushing against my ear. "Yeah."

Desire shivers down my spine. "Let's go."

Zero

I've finally met my match. Not that the girls who hang out at my MC aren't eager and willing. But holding an actual conversation with one can be rough. This girl. I almost want to *talk* to her as much as I want to fuck her.

Sex wins, but it's close and that's new for me.

Outside the bar, I reach over and take her hand without thinking. Dangerous move, maybe. She glances down at our intertwined fingers as if she's as surprised as I am.

She directs me to her house with a series of taps against my shoulder and somehow I find the secluded, wooded driveway. "You live here all by yourself?" I ask as soon as I shut the bike down.

"Yeah, you're safe," she teases.

Lights flood the front yard. "Motion sensors," she explains. "Don't worry, my dad's not waiting up for me or anything."

"So, this is your parent's house?"

She cocks her head and drills me with a serious stare. "No. It's mine. Bought and paid for it myself."

This seems important to her, so I nod. "Cool. I respect that." I do. I've worked hard for everything I have. Even if some of that work is outside the law. So I got respect for anyone who makes their own way.

Our feet crunch over the gravel drive. She's walking slow. I glance over and catch her watching her feet. "I usually park closer to the porch," she mutters. Shit, I hadn't been thinking about her heels and the uneven ground.

"Sorry." I pull her close and swing her up into my arms.

"Ahh!" she gasps and taps my chest. "Put me down."

"No way. This'll be quicker."

"Eager, huh?"

"Fuck yes."

When my foot hits her bottom step, I loosen my hold, allowing her to slide down my body in the most seductive way possible. She lands on the next step but keeps her arms looped around my neck so we're nose to nose. "You're charming for a biker thug."

"Don't get the wrong idea."

"I already have a lot of wrong ideas." She swoops in and presses her lips against mine. For a second, I'm too surprised to respond. Not used to chicks makin' the first move. My hands move first. Sliding right down her tight curves to squeeze her ass and pull her tight to me. She gasps and I use her surprise to take her mouth hard and urgent. After letting me have my way with her lips and tongue, she throws her head back, inviting me to taste her skin.

"You do this a lot, don't you?" she asks, breaking my concentration. "I bet the girls take one look at you and can't drop their panties fast enough." Her husky, raw voice fuzzes my brain so bad it takes a second for her words to sink in.

"You want me to ask the same question, sugar?" My voice has an edge to it—a mix of pissed off and turned the fuck on.

"Go ahead." She grins as if she thinks she's gonna beat me at some game.

"Shut up," I say instead and her smile widens. She's beautiful and cocky enough to make me think stupid things. My fingers twist into all her thick long, hair, pulling her against me for another taste of her mouth. Why'd her assumption bother me so much? Because it's true or because I want more than one night out of her? This time, I can't pry myself away. Eager, soft hands slide under my cut, slipping it down my shoulders. She pulls away to examine the leather.

"It's heavier than I thought," she whispers while tracing her fingers over the back patch. "Skull and crown. Oddly pretty." She folds it gently over her arm and leads me to her porch swing. She pushes me down into the swing, and it's strangely reminiscent of getting a lap dance. Except, I can touch her. So I do.

My hands skim up her sleek legs right up under her

dress. When my thumbs brush against the skinny string at her hip, I yank hard, snapping it and tearing the underwear from her.

Her husky laughter fills the air, teasing my dick. "You owe me a pair of panties now."

"I'll happily pay up." My fingers seek and stroke against her slick, bare skin and she hisses. I can't help but lean and kiss the area I'm touching. She gasps and twists her fingers in my hair.

Suddenly, I'm consumed with the need to see every inch of her body. Take my time. Explore and savor this woman. I've had enough quick, sweaty, anonymous hook-ups in the dark. "Let's go inside."

"It's fun on the porch swing." She steps back and slides her hands over her dress, putting everything in place. Well, everything but the panties I ripped off. Will it be too creepy of me to stuff them in my pocket and keep 'em as a trophy?

"I'm sure it is, but I'm not into getting mosquito bites on my balls."

That makes her laugh and back up a step. I use the space to push out of the swing and wrap my arms around her, lifting her against me.

At the door, she leans down and pushes it open.

"Don't you lock that?"

"No one locks their doors out here."

I shake my head. But I'll have to address her security needs later.

I twist the lock behind us before carrying her farther into the house.

Lilly

"Bedroom?"

"Guess," I tease and he groans.

His hand squeezes my ass and I almost wriggle out of his hold. "Careful, I don't want to drop you, sugar."

"I know you won't."

A smile tugs at the corner of his mouth. He has to be the most ridiculous combination of sexy, dangerous and impish, I've ever met.

Maybe one night with him is a bad idea. Except I can't possibly see there being anything else between us.

When he reaches my room, he sets me down next to my bed gently. Before I make another move, he tucks his finger under my chin and tips my head up to meet his winter-blue eyes. "You sure you still want this?"

"Be more specific."

His mouth twists into a wry smile. "You sure you still want my cock?"

"Oh, yes. You're not getting away now."

He grins even wider and slides his finger down my neck, over my collarbone to the edge of my dress. "Take this off."

Our eyes lock as I reach behind me to pull the zipper down and lower the dress. He doesn't back up even an inch, so I end up letting it drop to the floor and kicking it to the side.

"Keep going," he growls, just loud enough for me to make out the words.

"Not fair."

"Who said this was going to be fair?" His words are cocky, but his breathing has picked up.

I thrust my chin at him and cross my arms over my chest to stop the trembling. Guys don't usually make me nervous. "Lose the shirt." The words come out with more confidence than I'm actually feeling.

"I knew you were going to be fun," he mutters as he slips his T-shirt over his head and tosses it on top of my discarded dress. Oh, Jesus, that's nice. He's big. Everywhere. Rough, tattoos flowing over every inch of skin. Beautiful, intricate pieces of art that must have taken many hours to complete. He'd be intimidating except for the smile and dimples.

I raise an eyebrow and he chuckles. His hands work his belt loose, shoving his jeans down his legs. He falters for a second while he works his boots off, then pushes everything to the side.

His hand grips my hip, pulling me close, so his face can nuzzle my neck. His raspy cheek, rough against my skin.

"Your turn," he whispers.

Zero

The heat pouring off Lilly fucks with my head. But it's no match for her naked skin. Losing the dress almost makes me lose my mind. I have to step back so I can take all of her in.

I rub my hand over my chin, wiping away any stray traces of drool. "Fuck me, you must have made a fortune dancing."

She snorts. "That's a few years behind me."

Whatever. I'd hire her right this second…and end up beating every man who looked at her half to death.

"I don't like that you're comparing me to other—"

I stop her before she finishes the ridiculous thought. "Trust me, there's no comparison. Turn around."

She chuckles but complies. I'm glad she's facing away. Because my dropped-jaw expression probably makes me look like a dipwad who's never seen a naked chick in his life. But fucking hell, she's hot. Her hips curve perfectly to fit my hands as I yank her against me. My lips find her shoulder, kissing a path to her ear. "You're fucking perfection."

"Thank you."

Love her confidence. I'm so over chicks who offer weak denials when you pay them a compliment. She trembles as my hands make their way from her hips, to cup her tits. Also perfect. And real. Everything in me is screaming to get inside this woman, but still, I take my time. She leans against me and sighs. "I have condoms in the top drawer." She tips her head to the side toward her nightstand.

"Condoms, plural, huh?"

"Definitely." She reaches back and gives my cock a quick squeeze through my briefs. "I think the first time will be pretty quick."

I'm too amused to be insulted. Besides, she's probably right. Her breasts are still in my hands, and I squeeze gently, loving the feel of her soft, round flesh against my rough hands. Her nipples beg for my thumbs to brush over the stiff tips. She whimpers and arches her back, driving her ass right into my dick. Another second of this and I'll snap. My hand glides down her belly, then over her mound, fingers dipping between her thighs and along her slick lips.

"You want me?"

She replies by moaning and wiggling against my hand. Gasps when I find her opening and shove two fingers inside. "Spread your legs." I dip down to get a better angle as she does what I ask, and I'm loving the feel of her slick heat squeezing my fingers. My thumb brushes against her clit and she jolts. "You close?"

She hums and shakes her head.

"That's hot, but I need some words, Lilly. Tell me."

"No. Not yet."

Honesty. I like it.

"Get on the bed."

She turns and perches on the edge of the bed. Her hands dive for my underwear, tugging it down my legs, and she follows it to the floor. Kneeling in front of me, she glances up and smiles. One of her hands wraps around my cock, stroking a few times before taking me in her mouth.

"Fuck!" My hands tangle in her hair and I forget everything. Her tongue swirls over the tip while her hand strokes my shaft. "Fuck, that's good." She takes me deeper, gliding forward and back. Best head I've ever had. I'm much too close to the edge, and this isn't how I want things to go down. Reaching over, I snag open her drawer and yank out a condom. She keeps sucking, and licking right up until I've got the condom ready to roll down my dick, then pulls away with a smile on her face. "Get up on the bed."

She hops up on the bed and scoots back, resting on her elbows, knees wide. Hot as fuck. Especially with that secret smile curving her reddened lips. As I crawl up her body, she loops her arms around my neck. "I think you're the hottest man who's ever been in my bed."

I lower my mouth to kiss her. To shut her up because I don't want to think about her with anyone else. I thrust hard and she moans into my mouth. My hand cups her face, thumb brushing her cheek. I have to pound into her or die. She gasps, moans, then screams out a stream of sexy curses as she finds her release.

"You've got a filthy mouth, Lilly."

She sucks in a deep breath and her lips tilt into a satisfied smirk. "You've got a wicked cock." Her words are low and husky. They're my undoing.

A few short thrusts and my cock explodes. "Fuck!"

I roll to the side, taking her with me, pulling her close.

Kissing the top of her head, I brush her sweaty hair off her forehead and she smiles up at me. "Going to stick around for round two?"

"Absolutely."

She smiles even wider and, after a second, slips out from underneath me. "Be right back."

Too spent to move, I watch her sexy ass sway out of the room.

After I spot a wastebasket to toss the condom in, she still hasn't returned. Since we just met and all, I throw on my briefs before leaving the bedroom to find her. Because I'm a practical guy, I pluck a condom out of the nightstand drawer and tuck it in my waistband.

The house is dark, but a soft glow from the kitchen leads me to Lilly. As my feet touch the cold tile floor, she turns.

"Hey, I was just grabbing some water," she explains.

My mouth can't form any words. I'm too twisted from watching her stand casually naked in her kitchen. Instead, I walk up behind her, put my hands on her hips and yank her against me. The way her body softens against mine brings my lips to her shoulder. She shivers as I kiss my way to her ear. "Aren't you worried about someone spying on you?"

We are, after all, standing in front of her kitchen window. Except for the bedroom, none of her windows seem to have any coverings.

"No one's around for a few miles," she answers and I grin when I hear the quiver in her voice.

A second later, I'm laughing when she rubs her ass against my hardening dick. The friction knocks the little foil packet out of my waistband. Lilly reaches down and plucks it up off the floor.

She turns and faces me with a raised eyebrow. "Feeling hopeful?"

My shoulders lift. Can't help my grin from spreading. "Safety first."

"I like that."

Lucky me.

She loops her arms over my shoulders. Big brown eyes blink up at me. "What did you have in mind?"

"Haven't thought that far ahead." Behind her, I see she set out two glasses of water. "Were you bringing me water too?"

Her brow wrinkles in the cutest way. "Yes. Why?"

It's fuckin' sweet, that's why. I can already tell something's different about this encounter. About *this* woman.

"Thanks," I answer, reaching past her to grab one of the glasses and downing it in a few swallows.

She jumps when I thump the glass on the counter. "Come here."

"I'm already plastered against you. How much closer do you want to get?"

Fuck, that mouth of hers is a turn on.

I hook my arm tighter around her, pulling her closer. Our lips meet with no hesitation. We're touching at every point—our mouths, her soft breasts against my hard chest, but it's not enough. Obviously, she feels the same way because she claws at me, shoves her hands into my hair, holding me still. We're a frantic jumble as I back her out of the kitchen. No way can I make it all the way to her bedroom. She must agree because she pulls me into the living room, shoving my underwear down my hips before we even reach the couch.

"Turn around," I demand. "Let me see that ass again."

She smirks, but turns. Shakes her ass at me as she drapes herself over the end of the couch.

"Don't worry, sugar. I'm gonna fuck you."

Her low, throaty laugh gets me even harder and I struggle to rip open the condom packet and get it on. She arches and bounces up on her tiptoes, eager and playful. In a smooth thrust, I enter her. We both gasp and groan at the shock.

"Fuck," she moans, low and throaty. The sounds she makes set me off and I'm grabbing her like a wild fuckin' animal. Holding onto her hips, thrusting into her. She spasms and clenches around my cock, coming fast and hard.

She reaches back, wrapping her hands around my forearms. I'm fuckin' gone, my rhythm shot to hell, as I keep pounding into her. I can't help shouting as I push into her once, twice, then again as my orgasm takes over. The whole time, she's whispering filthy words of encouragement.

I slump over her back, careful not to crush her against the arm of the couch.

After a couple seconds, she wriggles until I stand, pulling her up with me.

Another one of her sexy smirks almost does me in.

"Maybe we should grab a nap before round three," she says with a teasing smile.

This can't be the only night I spend with Lilly. "Fuck yeah."

2

CHRISTMAS GIFT

This short story was originally published in
Three Kings, One Night (Lost Kings MC #2.5)

Zero

I shouldn't visit Lilly tonight.

Not on Christmas Eve.

She comes from a big, tight-knit family, so she's probably not even home.

It's fuckin' stupid for me to drive all the way up to see her. Especially if I just want to get laid.

I can do that back at the clubhouse.

Until half an hour ago, I'd been at my own awkward family dinner. My blood family, not the MC. Tricky business navigating the minefield of family relations around the holidays. Eventually, people drank too much and started listing all the ways you've disappointed them with the way you're living your life. I'd managed to stay until a physical unease built up so strong, it pushed me out the door.

Way too fucking cold to ride my bike, I'm trapped in my black truck, racing up the Northway.

To see a girl who may not want to see me. Who may not even be home. Or even worse, if she is home, might have some other guy over.

I do *not* like that idea.

At all.

I blame my best friend, Rock for my predicament. I'd never have met Lilly if he wasn't so damn obsessed with Lilly's friend—his former lawyer—Hope. Sweet as they come, Hope is the last woman you'd expect to find dating an MC president. Sometimes it shocks me she's managed to stay friends with Lilly for so long. All class and beauty on the outside, with the foulest mouth and an appetite for sex to match any man, Lilly keeps me on my toes.

She doesn't care if I fuck around with other chicks because she's fucking other guys.

First time this scenario has ever annoyed me.

Tonight I didn't bother calling first. Last time I went that route, she told me she was busy. I'm not giving her an out tonight.

I even have a present with me.

No, not my dick. That comes later.

Her driveway is dark, but that's not unusual. Christ, I

feel like a stalky dickwad. Her porch light is on, but her little Lexus sedan is nowhere to be seen.

Fuck.

I knew it was a risk coming all the way up here.

I'm still dicking around in her driveway, trying to decide if I should wait or head back down to Empire when headlights come bouncing down the driveway. I swear my dick pulses to life at the sight.

Lilly

I managed to hold back the tears until I got in my car. Over the years, I've learned nothing can pierce your heart more than family. At thirty-three, it is scandalous that I'm not married and carting a bunch of kids around with me. Never mind that I paid for college and graduate school all by myself. That I bought my own house before I turned thirty with my own money. That I haven't asked my parents for a dime since I left home.

If it wasn't for my older brother, Alex, playing mediator, I wouldn't have lasted through my mother's mushroom soup with *zaprashka*—the first of twelve miserable courses I sat through tonight. Even though my mother bent her traditions a long time ago, and now celebrates Christmas Eve on the 24th of December instead of January 7th, the meal she makes has not changed.

How badly I wanted to take comfort in the familiar

smells and tastes of my childhood. But once my mother got busy picking out my flaws and failures, it was only a matter of time before my father, aunts, and cousins joined the fun.

Lilly, when you gonna find a man to take care of you?

I can take care of myself, Babbo.

Nonsense, you're getting too old to attract a man.

Zia Bruna, I attract plenty of men.

That one had not gone over well. I'm pretty sure my family still thinks I'm a virgin.

I hate to break it to them, but that ship sailed a long time ago.

Why hadn't I moved farther away?

I could call my best friend, Sophie. Before her parents divorced, their strict expectations of her rivaled my own family's. But she's off in New Hampshire, spending the holiday with her rock star boyfriend who has some downtime until after New Year's.

After a quick stop at Stewart's, I have a quart of my favorite eggnog in my possession. When I get home, I'm going to introduce the eggnog to the bottle of Bailey's Irish Cream I have stashed in my fridge. Then I'm going to crawl into bed and forget that I have to get up and do this again tomorrow.

My heart jumps in my throat at the sight of a black SUV parked near my house. Nestled at the end of a long, bumpy driveway, my house is isolated—which is how I've always liked it. My foot slips off the accelerator as I process what I want to do. Turn around and drive away? Call 911? Call Alex?

Before I can do any of those things, the door swings open and a big, black-booted foot steps out.

Z.

My mouth quirks. I swear to God my nipples tighten and a slick rush of heat dampens my panties.

Christmas Eve just got a whole lot better.

Zero

"Z? What are you doing here?"

Her throaty voice gets me so fucking hard, my dick's banging against my zipper.

Showtime.

Snagging the package off the front seat, I meet her in the driveway.

"Wanted to give you your Christmas present."

She cocks her head in a way I don't find all that comforting. But her hand reaches out to take the bag. Before her fingers skim over the brown paper sack, I yank it away.

"Nu-uh. Not yet."

She plants a fist on her hip and gives me a cool stare that's hot as fuck. "You don't have to bring me presents if you want to get laid. You and your big cock are enough."

Raising my hand and flattening my palm over my heart, I answer her in a wounded voice. "What a sweet-talker. Now, are you gonna invite me in? It's so fuckin' cold I can see your nipples through your wool coat."

Her mouth twitches with a repressed grin. I'm gettin' to her. Next thing I know, she's standing flush against me, pushing me back in small steps until my back is against my car.

"Not so fast, sexy girl." Slapping the bag on the roof, I flip places and pin her up against the car door. Her mouth forms a small "o" of surprise, but I take it in a rough kiss before she gets out a sound.

Then her hands are in my hair, pulling me closer. My arms snake around her waist, holding her tight to me.

Fuck, I've missed this. No one tastes like Lilly. Smells like her. Feels like her.

So fucking good.

Breathlessly, she pulls away.

"Do you want to come inside?"

Hell, fucking, yes.

Lilly

This is nuts, but I don't care.

Breaking our kiss, I pull back as much as I can, trapped between Z's hard body and his truck.

"What's wrong, all your club whores go home for the holidays?"

He smirks, but a muscle tics at the corner of his eye. Maybe I offended him?

"Jealous, sexy girl?"

I flatten my palms over his chest with the intention of pushing him away, but I get distracted by the rock-hard muscles lurking under his warm, leather jacket.

I'm not wearing gloves so I curl my hands, trying to warm my fingers.

He leans down, soft lips brushing against my ear. Warm breath tickling against my neck. "Come on, sexy girl, invite me in."

A shiver that has nothing to do with the cold works over me. "I already did."

"Then let's go." Reaching over me, he grabs the little brown paper bag off his roof and takes my hand,

"Wait, I've got stuff in my car that I need to bring inside."

He waits while I grab my eggnog and the plate of cookies my aunt shoved into my hands before I left.

Once we're inside, I'm oddly nervous.

Z is the only guy I've ever known who makes me nervous.

After taking off our coats, I lead him into the kitchen so I can put the nog in the fridge and the cookies on the counter. Almost shyly, Z holds out the paper bag to me.

"Condoms? You know I keep plenty of those," I joke.

He doesn't laugh.

"Open it."

When I do, I almost cry, which is stupid. Inside is a canister of Godiva dark chocolate hot cocoa mix. "I can't believe you remembered. Where did you manage to find it?"

He shrugs casually, but his smile and the crinkle at the corners of his eyes tell me he's pleased with my reaction.

"You said it's the only kind of hot chocolate you like, and you have to have hot chocolate on Christmas Eve, it's mandatory."

"Yeah, but the Godiva store at the mall closed. Where did you even find it?"

He shakes his head. "I have my ways."

I'm not sure what to think of that. I know I'm probably reading too much into this, but the cocoa isn't easy to find, which means he went to some trouble to track down this gift. For me. When that's not what our relationship is about.

"Christ, Lilly, it's a beverage, not an engagement ring. Calm the fuck down."

"No, it's really sweet. Thank you."

He raises an eyebrow at me.

"You want me to make it now?" I ask him with a laugh.

"Well, yeah. You told me it was the greatest thing ever. I gotta see if it lives up to the hype."

This is getting weird quick. Z and I fuck. We don't sit around sipping hot chocolate together.

"Okay." Rolling up my sweater sleeves, I get to work. I pull out a small saucepan, my favorite whisk, and a half-gallon of milk.

I don't bother measuring anything out. I know from memory just how much of each ingredient to use.

Z's quiet while he watches me whisk the milk and powder together over low heat. "The key is to constantly stir the milk so it doesn't burn," I tell him over my shoulder to break the silence.

"See, I would never know that. I would have jacked the fire up and set the milk to boil."

I chuckle because I can picture him doing exactly that.

Taking down my favorite cocoa mugs, I stifle a laugh. Z's going to think I'm nuts.

At first, he doesn't notice but then he tips one mug to the side.

"Remington?"

I chuckle, a high-pitched sound that splits my ears. Why am I so *nervous* around him tonight? "They were a house-warming present from my brother. For situations just like this. You know, if I had a guy over, he'd find out quick that I've got a shotgun and a big brother."

Z throws his head back and laughs. "Yeah, I bet he's got a shovel too." He stops and looks at me a little more seriously. "He wouldn't like me at all, would he?"

"I don't know," I answer honestly. "Anyway, joke's on him. They're perfect cocoa mugs, 'cause they're so big and weighted just right. I use them all the time even though they're ugly as shit."

He chuckles as he watches me pour hot chocolate into each mug.

"No marshmallows?"

I wrinkle my nose at him. "Nope. Sorry." Stretching up

on tiptoes, I snag a bottle out of the cabinet where I stash my liquor. "How about marshmallow vodka?"

His nose actually wrinkles. "Sounds a little girly."

"Suit yourself."

"Oh, all right. Hit me," he asks, holding out his mug.

After taking a sip, he glances at me. "Not bad, Lilly, you're always so clever."

I hate how much the compliment excites me. But it does. I'm used to men complimenting my looks. More specifically, my boobs. But few men ever comment on my intellect.

Z does. And it's not the first time, either. He's sincere, too, which I appreciate. It's not like he has to sweet-talk his way into my bed.

Let's face it, the man has an all-access pass.

That thick dark hair of his just begs to have my fingers run through it. His eyes are especially stunning. Mischievous midnight blue is the best way to describe them.

He smiles, softening his dangerous good looks.

"I like when you smile," I say softly.

"Oh yeah?"

"Yeah, you've got these cute little dimples." I tap his cheek to emphasize my point and, as I'm pulling away, he captures my hand.

"Cute?"

The feel of his strong hand wrapped around mine sends electrifying sensations through me. Gazing into his dark blue eyes, I'm struck by how much I really *like* Z.

"I like cute, but I also like big, dangerous, and powerful."

"Am I those things too?"

"Yes."

His eyes simmer with heat, and I use my free hand to stroke his raspy cheek. He leans in and brushes his mouth against mine. So gentle for a man who looks so demanding. Releasing my hand, he wraps his arms around my body, pulling me tight against him.

He growls when I flick my tongue against his lips and deepens our kiss. The taste of chocolate is sweet as he glides his tongue into my mouth.

Zero

Normally, I'm not into being some good girl's bad boy experience. But despite all appearances, Lilly has never pretended to be a good girl.

Still, the fact that she finds me so dark and dangerous strokes my giant biker ego in all the right spots. Her luscious curves pressed tight against me are an extra bonus. My hands roam down to run over her perfectly round ass.

Pulling away, I take in her heavy-lidded expression. Just because I know where this night is headed, doesn't mean I don't want to enjoy the journey.

My gaze skips down to her dark green sweater. It sets off her almost black hair and brings out the green and gold flecks in her dark brown eyes.

"You look pretty tonight."

She arches an eyebrow at me. "What?" I ask. Most girls like compliments, but you can never tell with Lilly.

"Nothing, my mother was annoyed because I didn't dress up nicer."

Stepping back, I take in her outfit more carefully. Soft, fuzzy sweater, tight enough to accent her generous curves but loose enough to still be acceptable for a night with the family. Dark jeans and low-heeled boots. Small gold earrings glitter in the kitchen light when she tosses her head back. I'm not sure what Lilly's mother expected, but *I* certainly like what the sexy girl in my arms has goin' on.

"Well, I like it," I say as my hands find their way to her cheeks, my thumbs stroking along her jaw.

"Are you planning to spend the night?" she asks.

"Are you inviting me to or are you going to kick me out after you get yours?" I say it as a tease, but that's been the way it's gone down the last few times.

Color races up her neck into her cheeks. I had no idea Lilly was even capable of blushing.

"You can stay."

I pull her tight again and grind my hips against hers so she knows how much I want her. "Good, 'cause I want to fuck you more than once."

"So ambitious."

Lilly

A couple kisses from Z and I'm toast. Done.

I try sucking in a breath, but it's futile. He has me pinned against the counter. The warmth and hardness of his wonderful, muscular body sends my heart thumping wildly. His thick arms have me held captive and my panties are fucking soaked.

The heat this man stirs up inside of me is ridiculous.

And I just agreed to let him spend the night.

His face moves closer and he nuzzles my neck. His raspy cheek is rough against my skin and I love the feel. His lips brush against me, sending tingles dancing through me. Ah, God, his teeth nibbling at my ear lobe is going to be my undoing.

A soft sigh of pleasure escapes my lips and I sag against the counter for support. Too weak to even hold myself up under his sensual assault.

He chuckles against my ear. "I remember what you like, sexy girl."

Yes, he does.

His big, rough hands skim down my sides, then sneak under my sweater. "Should I undress you right here?"

He tickles my ribs but, instead of laughing, it makes me moan.

"Would you like me to fuck you hard and fast on your counter?"

Both hands are under my sweater but they stop just under my breasts. I make a needy, pleading noise and arch my back, wanting his hands.

"Or, I could take you over to your couch. Bend you

over the back and take you from behind." He punctuates the dirty image by thrusting his hips against me.

I can't take any more. I wrap my arms around his neck and tilt my head to the side, kissing him to get him to shut up. My hands stroke down his broad shoulders, over his chest, skip down over the bumps of his abs, finally landing on the impressive bulge in his jeans.

"I'll leave it up to you." I squeeze his dick just a little so he remembers what it feels like to have my hands on him.

"I don't even know where to start, Lilly. That's how fucking nuts you make me."

It's a sweet sentiment. A little filthy too. I could get used to this sweeter side of Z. I already like his filthy side.

His lips glide over my jaw and take my mouth again. My body won't stop trembling while his hands slide down over my ass again, this time pulling me up and into him. He breaks our kiss long enough to look in my eyes. "Wrap your legs around me, girl."

"I can't."

"Yes. You. Can. Do it. I got you."

Keeping his hands under my ass, he carries us into my bedroom and tosses me on my bed. It's messy and unmade, but it's not like Z has ever invited me to see his room at the clubhouse, so I really don't give a shit.

I prop myself up on my elbows to admire him. "Take your shirt off."

He grins, an irresistible flash of dimples, then slowly works his shirt off.

"Fuck," I groan.

A slower smile spreads over his face. "You like that, huh?"

Sinking my teeth into my lower lip, I can only nod. Why do I only seriously date older men again?

Money. Security. But none of that seems important as I gaze at Z's perfectly chiseled and tattooed body posing before me. Yes, he's a cocky fucker, but he's earned it. He looks damn good and I don't blame him one bit for being proud of it.

He unzips his pants and steps out of them. "Why are you still dressed?"

Kneeling up on the bed, I pull my sweater over my head and toss it at him.

"That's better. God damn your tits are perfect." He reaches to run a finger over my black, see-through bra, pausing to tease my nipples into hard points. "Fuck, that's sexy. Were you planning to get fucked tonight?" he asks with a bit of an edge to his voice.

Narrowing my eyes, I brush his hand off me. "What kind of question is that?"

He thrusts his chin at me. "The sexy underwear."

A soft chuckle escapes me. "That's all I own."

"Fuck."

"No granny panties in my drawers." I continue, provoking him.

He lets out a strangled groan while rubbing his hand over his neck and jaw. His gaze is glued to my body and a surge of feminine pride zips through me.

Hooking my thumbs under the straps of my bra, I

tease them on and off my shoulders. "This is tame."

"Lilly," he warns before diving onto the mattress with me. He's all business as his hands go straight for the button on my jeans. He tugs and jerks the material down my legs, then tosses them on the floor. A conflicted look crosses his face.

"I don't know where to start first."

His sincerity makes me chuckle. "Come here and kiss me."

Gently, he lowers himself over me. The warmth of him soaking into me. The weight of his muscular body pressing me into the mattress. One hand glides down, stroking over my panties, then pushing them aside to run his fingers over my slick folds.

One finger pushes inside and my head rolls to the side. My hips arch up, seeking more of his soft, focused, exploratory touches.

"Sexy girl's fuckin' soaked," he whispers against my ear.

I nod my head frantically. Then my whole body jerks when he scrapes his teeth over the tip of my nipple. The thin material of my bra does nothing to dull the sensation of his warm, wet mouth closing over my breast.

"Ahhh...Z."

My other breast gets the same treatment until I'm squirming and damn close to begging for his cock.

"Z, please."

I feel, rather than see, the smirk he's wearing, but he

doesn't answer me, just keeps taking his sweet time licking and tasting me.

It's going to take a little more persuasion on my part, so I curl my fingers into the waistband of his boxer-briefs and tug.

"Wait," he growls.

"I can't." In this moment, I'm not ashamed at all. I'm too desperate to have his iron hard cock gliding into me to care that I'm begging.

Thankfully, he takes pity on me. Lifting his head, looking around the room as if he's as disoriented as I am, he hones in on my nightstand and reaches to grab the condoms he knows I store in the top drawer.

There's no fumbling. Every movement is deliberate, sure, and sexy as hell. He kicks out of his briefs, and hooks his arm under my knee, spreading me wide. His thumb teases against my clit, rubbing in gentle circles for a second before sliding his cock down the length of my slit. Even through the condom, I feel how hot he is. Burning up, just like me. When I think I'm going to scream from frustration, he places his cock at my opening and pushes inside, so fucking slow.

The best kind of torture.

Zero

The way Lilly stares up at me while I'm pressing inside her melting hot pussy is enough to make me lose it. But I hold on because I want this to be good for both of us. Her throaty voice in my ear is so fuckin' sexy as I pull back a bit. She's so fucking hot and wet, squeezing me so good.

I thrust in deeper and she cries out. Her sharp nails rake down my shoulders. "Harder. More. Please." Each word comes out in a sexy, panting breath.

"Hang on, baby, I'm gonna give you more than you can handle."

I slide out, then thrust in harder. Over and over, jiggling her amazing tits, slamming her bed into the wall. Her nails dig in deep and I love it.

"Z, I need...I need..."

"I know. Hang on, this feels too good to stop."

But I do stop, long enough to flip us.

"Oh God, yes." Her eyes practically glow in the light of the moon coming in through her bedroom window. She lowers herself onto me, so fast she ends up gasping and raising herself right back up. I can't help chuckling.

"Easy, girl."

Lilly likes a challenge, and she guides my dick into her hot pussy once more, this time easing herself down slower. Squeezing every inch of me as she takes me inside her body.

"Fuck, that's good, Lilly. Right there."

She rakes her nails down my chest and I arch up, driving my cock deeper. The primal groan she lets out makes me feel like a fucking rock star. Reaching up, I draw the straps of her bra down, freeing her perfect, round breasts, then cupping them in my hands. She throws her head back, the ends of her hair tickling against my thighs. Pinching her nipples a bit, I arch up again.

"Fuck me, girl."

She tips her head down, a lopsided smile lights up her pretty face. "Yes, sir."

Oh, fuck. "Don't start that shit." I laugh.

She lifts her body, then lowers. Rocks up and down, squeezing the fuck out of my dick. I let her have her way with me until she's moaning with pleasure, slamming herself down and grinding her pelvis into me. "Fuuuck, that's so good, Z."

Yes it is.

I grab her hips and move her, thrusting up each time I yank her down. "Come for me, Lilly."

"I…" She never finishes. She gasps and moans. Deep, guttural moans that break apart and turn to screams. Raw, honest sounds, unlike any other woman I've ever been with.

That's it. Can't take any more. I roll her under me and pin her wrists over her head with one hand, thrusting into her hard. Her head rolls to the side, but her hips bump up to meet me thrust for thrust. Her legs tighten around my waist. Suddenly, I'm consumed with the need to have her eyes on me. I need her to see who's fucking her into oblivion.

I cup her face with one hand, turning her to me. "Look at me."

Her eyes pop open, and we stare at each other. She fights to free her hands, but I keep her pinned down. I love how she struggles beneath me and the way her eyes never leave my face. Even when she gasps again, cries out.

My cock can't take any more. I explode inside her with such force I'm surprised her head's still attached to her body. She slides into another orgasm and I keep thrusting, loving each ecstatic moan. Finally, I have to stop. I barely manage to roll over and drop the condom in the little basket by her bed.

It's Lilly who pulls me close to her body. That's new and I like it a lot. Her breath swirls across my chest. She nuzzles her cheek against me and sighs. "Merry Christmas."

Lilly

Big, warm arms hold me tight. Opening my eyes, I blink at the daylight and glance down at the heavily-tattooed arm wrapped around me.

Z.

Content, I sigh and relax against him.

"Morning," he rumbles from behind me.

Wriggling against him, I murmur my own good morning. Rough fingers trace up my arm, teasing my hair over my shoulder. His stubbly cheek rubs over my back, firm lips blaze a trail up my neck behind my ear.

Loud thumping from the living room startles us apart.

"The fuck?" Z snarls, reaching for his clothes and most likely a gun.

Bracing a hand on his shoulder, I listen carefully.

"Lilly!" comes the muffled shout.

Fuck!

Z scowls at me. "You expectin' someone, sweetheart?"

"No."

But I should have expected this. My brother, Alex, always stops by on Christmas morning to give me a pep talk before we head to my parents'. This is the worst. He's already seen Z's truck parked in my driveway and will have a million questions for me.

Fuck.

Throwing back the covers, I scurry around the room throwing on clothes so I can go greet my brother.

Zero

What the motherfuck?

What the motherfuck?

I was about to have myself a very nice Christmas morning fuck. My cock is throbbing at the thought of sinking back inside Lilly. But she's racing around the room like a nut.

'Cause there's another dude at her front door.

I don't believe this shit.

Neither of us want to be exclusive. We've had that talk. This arrangement suits me perfectly.

So why am I so fuckin' pissed right now?

At least I got here first.

Whoever's out there sounds just as pissed. Worried about my girl, I throw on my jeans and decide to put on a good show for her visitor.

I throw open her bedroom door and storm down the hallway. Bracing myself in the doorway to her living room, I feign a casual pose and assess my competition. Big, blond fucker. Well over six feet. My age, maybe older. I can handle him. Or at least get some good hits in trying.

"Lilly, darlin' I wasn't done with you yet," I slip the words out slowly and watch the guy's face turn red with rage.

Tough shit, fucker.

Lilly gasps. "Z, dammit."

Lilly's cheeks are pink as she ducks her face into her open palms. "Fuck, fuck, fuck," she mutters over and over.

The dude's hands are fisted at his sides.

"Who is your friend, Lil?"

She finally tips her head up, glaring at the guy. "Knock it off, Alex. That's what you get for barging in without calling."

"I did call you, like a hundred times."

"Oh, shit. My cell phone's in my car."

She's hesitating. Can't blame her. As pissed as I am, I recognize this must be real fuckin' awkward for Lilly.

She glances at me again and shakes her head. "Z, this is my *brother*, Alex. Alex, this is my friend, Z."

Friend, huh. Guess it sounds better than 'fuck buddy.'

So, this is her brother? I always pictured the dude with dark hair, like Lilly. Suddenly I'm feeling pretty fuckin' stupid standing here half-naked, trying to intimidate this guy.

Her brother. Shit.

Trying to smooth over the awkward moment, I step forward and raise my hand. "Hey, Alex."

Lilly's wide, pleading eyes are clearly saying, 'please put some fuckin' clothes on.'

Alex nods at me, but doesn't say anything.

"I, uh, I'll be right back."

Lilly

Even though I try to distract Alex by pulling him into the kitchen, his eyes bug out when Z turns around, and Alex gets a good look at the Lost Kings MC tattoo, taking up Z's entire back. While I find it incredibly sexy, Alex looks like he's going to have a stroke.

As soon as Z's out of eyesight, Alex grips my arm.

"Some motorcycle gang thug? Are you out of your fucking mind, Lilly?"

"He's not a thug. It's a motorcycle club, *big brother*."

"Jesus fuckin' Christ. He fuckin' hurts you, I'll kill him, and I'll have all his club brothers after me. Great."

"Knock it off. It's not like that."

I busy myself by making coffee. I'm mortified Alex caught me in this position. Not that he labors under any delusions about me, but still, this is awkward. Almost as awkward as when I found him and Sophie screwing each other after our senior prom.

"Like hell it's not. How long has this been going on? Where did you even meet someone like that?"

Now I'm pissed. He doesn't even know Z and he's judging him a little too harshly for my taste. I get the whole overprotective big brother thing, but this is too much. Besides the awesome orgasms, Z's always been rather sweet to me. While our relationship is strictly fuck-and-go, Z never makes me feel cheap or used. Something I can't say about a lot of the guys I've been with, so my brother's assumptions about Z's character based on a fucking tattoo tick me off.

"Do you really want me to answer those questions? We hook up from time to time, does that make you happy? I met him through a friend. He's a nice guy. I like him so stop being rude."

Alex sighs and runs his hands through his hair. "Fine. Damn, Lilly. I just worry about you. I was worried about you last night after that shitshow with Mom and Dad and Aunt Bruna's stupid mouth." He points to the box of cinnamon buns on the counter. "I brought these over to cheer you up before we have to go back and do it all over again. I didn't expect you to have *company*."

That's our Christmas ritual—cinnamon buns and coffee before family time. Shit, if my brain wasn't in my vagina, I would have remembered.

"Sorry, he stopped by unexpectedly to bring me a present and—"

Alex quirks an eyebrow at the word present, but we're interrupted by Z returning to the room.

Zero

Brother or not, hearing this dude hassling Lilly for being with me makes me want to beat the shit out of him. I get it, I do. If I had a sister and found some shady dude like me in her house, I'd probably react the same way.

But she's thirty-something years old. If she wants to have a fuck buddy over, that's her business and I don't appreciate her brother trying to make her feel bad about it. Then Lilly sticks up for me. Holy shit. I can't even say what I'm feeling hearing those fuckin' words comin' outta her mouth.

He's a nice guy. I like him—

If only she knew how *not* a nice guy I really am.

Now I'm hard as a rock, and probably shouldn't go back out there until I calm down.

When I finally make it back into the living room, I plan to head straight for the front door. "Hey, Lilly, I'm gonna—"

She glances at me with wide eyes. Fuck. "Stay. Have some cinnamon buns and coffee before you go?"

My eyes skip to her brother, but he's got his back to me, busy arranging something on a plate. Probably shoving rat poison in my cinnamon bun.

"Sure, if I'm not interrupt—"

A big fuckin' smile lights up her face and I'm so done

for. "You're not." She turns and bumps her brother out of the way and grabs the plate of pastries.

Setting them down on the table, she gestures for me to take a seat. It's awkward, but I snag a chair and plop myself into it while she runs back to the kitchen. Her brother sits across from me and meets my stare head-on. Brave fucker. Maybe I should ask him to prospect for us.

Inside, I'm laughing at the thought, but it must show on my face.

"Something amuse you?" Alex asks.

"Yeah, I was thinking you got big balls, throwing that attitude at a *thug* like me."

He doesn't react. Or at least he doesn't react the way I expect him to. He laughs. "I could say the same thing, you know."

"Can you guys do your whole pissing match thing some other time?" Lilly asks sweetly as she sets out three coffee mugs and one of those insulated coffee pots on the table.

Alex pats her hand and thanks her for the coffee. At least the dude is polite to his sister.

Lilly takes her place at the head of the table and shines a beautiful smile at both of us before slipping, warm, sticky rolls on each of our plates.

"Merry Christmas, guys."

3

———————

PERFECT BLEND

Brand new and previously unpublished.
For my regular readers of the series, in the LOKI timeline this
story takes place during
Strength From Loyalty.

LILLY

"I CAN'T BELIEVE she's really getting married again," Sophie says.

I tap my pen against the legal pad I'd been scribbling on before she called. "Why? If anyone deserves happiness, it's Hope."

"I know. I didn't mean otherwise." Her tone is less than convincing.

Sophie's been my best friend for as long as I can remember. My partner in crime throughout our rebellious teenage years. We put some distance between us while I worked toward my Master's and she was in law school. But that was survival instinct and not a comment on our friendship.

She and Hope have been friends since law school and I've grown closer to Hope since then. Jealousy seems to color most of Sophie's comments about Hope lately, and I can't quite figure out why. The woman's endured more heartache than most over the last few years. I meant what I said; she deserves to be happy.

"Didn't you orchestrate the two of them getting together in the first place?" I remind her.

"Well, yeah. But I didn't think he'd try to marry her. I don't want to see her get hurt again."

What to say here? Hope's an adult? Mind your own damn business? I'm not sure. "The man seems to worship the ground she walks on, Sophie. I think she'll be fine."

"Well, I'll have to meet you guys at Hamilton's. I can't leave here until six."

"That's fine. Mara's meeting me here."

Sophie's silent and I can almost picture her pouting. I'm not sure why she ever introduced me to her friends if she was going to be jealous every time I met up with them without her. "What are you wearing?" she asks.

I glance down at the teal blouse and mid-length, A-line, charcoal tweed skirt I picked out this morning. Normally on Thursdays and Fridays, we could wear whatever we wanted to the office. Sometimes I chose jeans. Usually, I tried to still dress somewhat professional.

Since it's near the end of the legislative session and a budget still hasn't been passed—nothing new there—there is always a chance I'd have to meet with one of the legislators I worked for so I'd chosen my outfit carefully.

"The same thing I wore to work. Blouse and a skirt."

She sighs. "Aren't you hoping to run into Z again?"

Hoping or dreading. I'm not quite sure. The sexy biker stirred up all sorts of crazy emotions every time I saw him. "I doubt he'll show up."

Besides, I plan to trade my gray sweater cardigan for a black leather jacket and my plain black pumps for a pair of teal, suede T-strap heels. That should dial down the nerdy professional look to something more bar-appropriate. Not that it matters. Even if Z shows up for some reason, he's always more interested in getting me *out* of my clothes than admiring them.

"I don't know about that," Sophie says.

"What about you? Is Jonny home this weekend?"

"I don't want to talk about him."

"Shit, I'm sorry."

"It's nothing. We can talk about it another time. I don't want to be a downer. We're supposed to be celebrating tonight."

Well, that's an improvement over how petty she was being earlier. "All right."

"Knock, knock," Mara sing-songs from outside my office door. I wave her in.

"Mara just got here. I'll see you in a bit?"

"Sure, sure. Go have fun without me."

I roll my eyes. "We'll see you soon."

Shaking my head, I hang up and smile at Mara. "Am I running late?"

"Nope, I was just so excited to get out of the house, I jetted out the door early."

"I'm shocked you even found my office." Legislative personnel were spread all over the Empire State Plaza. My office was situated between the Senate and Assembly, but still wasn't easy to find.

"I looked you up in Damon's handy directory."

"Oh." I laugh and stand. "Should've thought of that." I run my gaze over her maroon sweater and black dress pants. "You look pretty."

"Thank you." She runs her hands over her hips. "I don't think I'll ever recover from having Cora."

I snort and toss a small plastic bag at her. "I'd actually consider having kids if I knew I'd look as good as you a few months later."

"That's sweet. Thank you." She pokes through the bag and giggles. "Hope's going to die of embarrassment."

I grin at her. "We're celebrating her engagement. It's our obligation to give her dirty gifts."

Mara snaps her giant black leather purse open and pulls out a small paddle. "My thoughts exactly."

"Oh my God." Uncontrollable laughter spills out of me. "She really might die of embarrassment. We're the worst."

"What?" She raises her eyebrows in an innocent way, in complete contrast to her teasing smile. "Rock seems like a man with a firm hand. It probably needs a break."

I drop into my chair and laugh until tears run down my cheeks. "You bitch. Now I have to go fix my makeup."

I gather all my stuff and we head downstairs where I stop to reapply some eye-makeup.

"Hoping to see someone?" Mara asks, wiggling her eyebrows.

"You never know." I glance over at her. "Why?"

"Come on. Every time you see, which one is he, Z, right? Your panties hit the floor with a thud."

"A thud, huh?"

"I was trying to be dainty."

"You can't be *dainty* when you're discussing someone's panties hitting the floor."

"A-ha!" She points one perfectly manicured fingernail in my direction. "See, you don't deny it."

I close my eyes and wait until I stop shaking with laughter before continuing to run the mascara brush over my lashes. "I'm going to end up with smudges all over the place if you keep that up."

She sets a blinding hot-pink gift bag on the counter next to us and pulls out a few sheets of tissue paper. "Look at you, all prepared."

"Nothing but the best for our girl." She squeezes her hands together under her chin. "I'm really happy for her."

"Me too." I may not be the marrying kind, but Hope is, and after all she's been through, I'm happy she found someone who treats her so well.

Mara wraps up the few gifts—all sex-related—while I finish my makeup.

"Are we walking or driving?" she asks.

I glance down at my heels. "Let's drive. I don't want to have to walk to the parking garage later by myself."

She elbows me in the side. "Oh, I'm sure a hunky biker or two will be more than happy to escort you to your vehicle."

True. Rock's protectiveness extends to Hope's friends. Not to mention, if Z shows up, he'd never let me wander the streets of Empire by myself.

"Even so, it's early so we should be able to find parking on Hamilton Street."

"If you're drinking, you can stay at our place again."

I glance over. "Are you sure about that?"

"Damon finds you extremely entertaining."

"Oh, I bet he does." I snicker and she *whaps* me with her purse. "Ow, what are you carrying in there, bricks?"

"Evening, Lilly. Headed home?" Someone calls out.

I barely hold back my groan of annoyance. Shane Kelly, one of the legislators I technically work for, leers at me from the security guard's station. "Evening, Assemblyman Kelley." I nod and force a polite smile. His reptilian gaze oozes over my body, then slides to Mara. She stiffens her spine and marches right up to him.

"Assemblyman Kelley. Mara Oak. I've heard so much about you from my husband."

Damon's reputation as a tough judge who doesn't sweep high-profile cases under the rug has ruffled many feathers. A few legislators who've been caught drinking and driving haven't gotten the usual special treatment they received before Damon took the bench. Something that, after working with these jackasses for so long, gives me endless pleasure.

"Good to meet you, Mrs. Oak."

"Well, we're late. Good evening." Mara loops her arm through mine and tugs me down the hallway to the elevator leading down to the garage. "Goodness, he's creepy."

"He wields a lot of power around here, though. Been in office since before I was born, probably."

She snort-giggles. "Probably." She lowers her voice. "Don't say anything, but Damon's thinking of running for Gold's seat if he runs for Senate."

"Good for him. Although, that's too bad because I've heard good things about him down at the city court."

"Nothing's set in stone. Now, hurry up. I want to get there before Hope."

"Hope's never on time. I'm sure we'll be there long before her."

She taps her temple and rolls her eyes. "Right, what was I thinking?"

Zero

"So, uh, what time are you going downtown to pick up your girl?" My question didn't come out as casually as I intended and Rock raises an eyebrow at me.

"Around ten-thirty." He casts a look Sparky's way. "If we ever finish up here."

We rode down into the commercial area of Empire to pick up some supplies for Sparky's plants. By the way our stoner brother's running around the small hydroponics shop, tossing stuff into a cart as he goes, it looks like we should've brought a truck.

"Boss! Boss, these are great!" Sparky's bloodshot eyes shift right and left. "The *to-ma-toes* will benefit from an additional light source."

Rock smothers a laugh with one leather-gloved hand. "Whatever you need, brother. Should we call Rav and ask him to bring the van?"

Sparky glances down at the pile of equipment scattered around his feet. "That's probably best."

The owner of the shop knows us well. We drop a fair amount of cash here on a regular basis, so he's not concerned or surprised by Sparky's antics.

An hour later, Ravage pulls the van into the parking lot and Sparky decides he's finally finished. Rock hands over a wad of cash to cover everything and the owner helps us load our goods into the van.

"You solid, brother?" I ask Sparky. We've been away from the clubhouse for a good three hours now. Can't remember the last time he set down the bong this long.

Sure enough, he twitches and glances at his bike. "Ready to head home."

"All right." Rock lightly punches Sparky's shoulder. "Go easy. The plants aren't going anywhere."

"I got you, boss." Sparky grins his loveably doofy smile and holds out his fist. "Shiny side up, brother." He taps Rock's fist, then mine, and finally Stash's before straddling his bike.

"Buddha help me," Rock mutters.

Wrath pounces on us at the clubhouse. Twitchy, I suppose, since Trinity went out to celebrate with the girls. "How long does it take to buy lights?" he grumbles.

"Bro, you have no idea. We've got high-output energy-efficient lights, spectra lights, LED lights, full spectrum lights. Not to mention, some bucket system hydroponic thing he wants to try out—"

"You'll thank me later, Zero!" Sparky shouts as he bounds down the stairs.

Wrath shakes with laughter. "Not sorry I missed that. At all."

"You're going next time," Rock says from behind me. "Your cast will be off by then."

"What for? If anyone should go, it's Teller. He's the money guy."

"Good call," Rock says. "Remind me next time."

I follow Rock into the war room with Wrath right behind me.

Rock glances over his shoulder. "Why do I have two shadows?"

"When are you heading downtown?" Wrath asks.

"You too?" Rock grumbles.

Wrath—*the dick*—smirks at me. "Aw, did you already bugging Prez about tagging along?"

"Shut up."

"Ten-thirty, unless she or Trin text earlier."

"Cool." I tap my fingers against the table as if I don't care one way or another. "I'll ride with you."

"Me too," Wrath adds. "Trin will drive me back."

"You hope so." I can't help but mess with Wrath. He and Trinity need to get their shit together.

Rock runs his hands through his hair and glares at both of us.

"What?" A sly smile spreads over my face and I wink at Wrath. "If you need to pull over and be 'alone' with your girl on the way home, I promise not to peek."

Wrath busts out laughing. "Nah, twenty bucks says Hope gets hammered off half a margarita and Rock has to carry her upstairs."

"You're not hoping to get a ride with Lilly?" Rock asks, ignoring Wrath's bet.

"No, he wants to give *her* a ride, Prez." Wrath snickers at his joke. "On his—"

"Yeah, I got it." Rock holds up a hand. "Christ."

An hour later, we're in Rock's SUV headed downtown, still bantering like brothers. Well, more like Wrath and I are heckling Rock. He is, after all, the oldest brother, and therefore gets the most abuse from us.

"You worried about her hanging with Sophie?" Wrath

asks Rock in a low voice. Sophie is Lilly's best friend so I perk up at her name.

"Nah, if she was going to say something, she woulda said it by now."

"You should tell her," Wrath says. "She sounds like a two-faced bitch. Hope doesn't need that in her life."

"Aw, look at you defending Hope when a few months ago, you were trying to chase her away," I tease.

"Shut up." Wrath reaches back to smack me, but I duck out range.

"That cast is slowing down all your reflexes," I taunt.

He twists and turns his big, bulky body and almost grasps my ankle.

"Do you two need to go back to high school?" Rock asks in a bored tone. He reaches over and wraps his hand around Wrath's forearm, squeezing hard enough to get his attention. "Simmer down."

"He started it."

"Jesus." He makes the final turn down narrow, one-way Hamilton street, cursing as we hit about fifteen different potholes. "I hate downtown."

"There's a spot right in front." I point.

Rock smacks my hand away from his face. "I'm not fucking blind. I see it, jackass."

"You're really dying to see this chick, huh?" Wrath asks me.

"I don't want to drive around the block all night looking for a spot. That's all."

"Yeah," Rock says in a dry tone, clearly not buying my bullshit. "Okay."

Lilly

Hope turned about as pink as her dress when we gave her the bag of goodies. Mara high-fived me and we giggled like schoolgirls.

Sophie—I'm not sure what to do about her. She drank way too much way too fast and has said a number of obnoxious things. Hope's friend, Trinity, keeps eyeing Sophie like she's waiting for an opportunity to slap the shit out of her.

When I have a moment, I elbow Sophie in the ribs. "What's gotten into you?"

"A lot of vodka." She grins at me and holds up her glass.

"No shit. Knock it off."

Hope's toast. She claims she had two margaritas, but I'm pretty sure she's counting the same glass twice. She's always been a lightweight. "You need to sober up so you can use those toys," I say.

She gives me a glassy-eyed smile. "I don't need toys." She holds her hands about two feet apart. "My fiancé has a huge—"

Mara bursts into giggles. "I *knew* it!"

"Who has a huge cock?" Mara's friend, Ross, asks.

Hope tries to point to herself but almost falls out of her chair. "My husband."

Trinity rolls her eyes and shakes her head. "Rock's gonna need that paddle tonight," she mutters.

Hope leans over like she has a secret to share with the table and points at Trinity. "Her boyfriend has got to be hung like a *moose*."

Trinity's cheeks flame red. "He's *not* my boyfriend."

"But he *is* hung like a moose?" Ross asks. "Just to clarify."

"He's your *moosefriend*." Mara giggles.

Even Trinity's laughing now. "That makes no sense."

"Tell Princess Bubble Yum over there," Mara says, pointing at Hope's blinding pink dress. "Hey, wake her up."

"Has she always been like this?" Trinity asks Mara.

"Can't hold her tequila?" Mara hiccups. "Yup."

Eventually, Hope sobers up a little. Just in time for Rock to join the party. The two of them are disgustingly sweet together. As hard as I try not to look at the door, searching to see if Z came with his friend, my gaze strays. I'm not disappointed when he joins us a few seconds later.

"How you been, pretty girl?" he asks against my ear as soon as he gets close enough.

Maybe I've had too much to drink. I swear his voice vibrates right down to my toes.

"Thud!" Mara yelps.

I shoot a glare at her and she laughs even louder. Thankfully, no one else knows what she's babbling about.

"Hi, Z," Sophie slides closer and wiggles her fingers at him. "You look good."

"How you doing, Sophie?" he asks with just enough interest to be polite, but not flirtatious.

Why should I care if he flirted with Sophie anyway?

I reach for my glass and down the rest of my drink. Z gives me a more careful look. "Are you driving home?"

"My car's outside." That doesn't really answer the question.

"I'll take you home." He leans in closer. "Or you can come home with me."

"I'm still over at my parking garage." Sophie gestures wildly in the direction of her office building.

"You don't look like you're in any condition to drive," Z says.

Am I terrible for wishing Sophie hadn't gotten drunk so I could be alone with Z? For being a little annoyed with her for so desperately trying to grab his attention when she knows we have…well, whatever we have.

Mara, Rock, Hope, and Trinity have already ventured outside. I wanted to have a second alone with Z, but Sophie doesn't seem to be leaving any time soon.

"I'm fine." Sophie slams back the rest of her drink and wobbles to her feet. "Unless you want to extend the invitation?" She wiggles her eyebrows and my hands tighten into fists under the table.

She's drunk. She's not doing it on purpose.

"We've been *there* before, right Lil?" She bumps into my shoulder and I push her away.

"Cut it out."

Sophie waves her finger in my direction. "She looks all professional now. But she was a wild girl back in the day."

"I believe you," Z says in a calm tone. Not the leering way I think Sophie was trying to coax out of him.

"You girls all right?" Ross asks.

"I got 'em," Z answers. He stands and holds his hand out to me. "Come on, let's get her home."

"I don't want to go home." Sophie pouts.

"You'll be unconscious by the time we get on the Northway."

I lean under the table and grab my bag and purse. Z watches and takes both out of my hands when I sit up.

"You don't have to do that."

"It's fine. Come on. I'll drive you home."

"Then how are *you* going to get home?"

He leans in, brushing his lips against my ear, sending shivers down to my nipples. "Maybe a certain pretty girl will invite me to stay?"

"Maybe." I pull back and he shifts his gaze to Sophie. His way, I think, of saying let's deal with her first.

Outside, we say a quick goodnight to everyone and head toward my car.

Z pulls my keys out of my hand as we get closer.

"Take us up to the clubhouse, Z," Sophie begs, attempting to jump on Z's back.

"Not tonight, ladies." He carefully slides her off of his back and steadies her before she falls over.

"I thought you were more fun." Sophie pouts.

He holds the back door open for her. "Try not to barf back there." Shaking his head, he walks around to the other side and opens my door. "You feel all right?"

"I didn't drink close to the amount she did."

"Good."

I lift my foot to step into the car and Z stops me with a hand around my waist. "You look pretty. Is this what you wore to work today?"

My cheeks burn with pleasure. "Changed my shoes. And jacket."

"I should visit you down here more often."

My heart skips. What would that look like? Would I take him to my favorite spot for lunch? Introduce him to my colleagues? Would he even want me to?

I think Z assumes my hesitation means I'd be embarrassed to be seen with him and he pulls away. "Never mind."

"No." I curl my fingers around his arm, holding him in place. "Friday afternoons are usually the easiest for me to take a long lunch."

His eyes widen. "Yeah?"

"Yeah," I whisper.

"I don't feel so good!" Sophie yells from the backseat.

I groan and slide into the car while Z chuckles.

Zero

"So where are we going next?" Sophie asks, popping up and resting her hand on my shoulder.

"We're taking you home." I brush her hand off my shoulder.

"Really?" Her high-pitched girlish voice cuts through the air like a knife. Isn't she the same age as Hope and Lilly? Shit, this chick is annoying. "You're going to have fun without me?"

"Taking Lilly home right after you."

I glance over, but Lilly's staring out the window.

"What happened to us, Lilly?" Sophie reaches up front and shakes Lilly's shoulder. "We were so much more adventurous in high school, remember?"

"I remember."

"Our parents used to send us to dance classes all the way down in Empire. And get this, Z." Sophie taps my shoulder harder and laughs loudly in my ear. "When we were old enough to drive, we just stopped going! We'd go meet boys instead. They were so pissed when they found out."

"Yes, they were," Lilly mutters.

"You were quite a badass, huh?" I tease.

Lilly shrugs, clearly uncomfortable with this topic. It's harmless enough, but it seems to bother her so I try to change the subject. "You gonna be able to get your car out of the garage tomorrow, Sophie? Or do they close for the whole weekend?"

"Nah, a lot of the associates work on the weekend, I'll be able to get it."

"I'll drive you down," Lilly offers.

The drive to Sophie's place seems to take forever. I've never been so happy to see Exit 9 in my life.

In the driveway, I leave the car running and let Lilly help her friend inside. Kinda makes me feel like a dick, but I don't want to drag this out longer than necessary either.

Twenty minutes later, Lilly hurries back to the car. "Sorry," she says as soon as she opens the door.

"Everything okay?"

"Should be. I called her brother to make sure he checks on her in the morning."

"You called him at this hour?"

"He works nights."

"Oh."

She's quiet while I navigate back to the highway. "Where we going?" I finally ask.

"I thought you wanted to take me to the clubhouse?"

"You want to come?"

As an answer, she slides her hand over my thigh and squeezes. "Why, yes, I do."

"Don't start that game, girl."

"What game is that?"

I glance over and find her biting her lip.

"The I'll-pull-over-and-fuck-you-right-now game."

She shifts and checks out the back seat. "There isn't enough room back there."

"I know for a fact you're quite flexible." I glance over again. "You sure you're sober?"

"Why? Because you wouldn't want to take advantage?"

"Yeah, exactly that." I reach over and settle my hand on her knee, gently stroking her skin. She shifts and parts her legs, inviting me to travel farther up.

She sighs and rests her head against the seat. "Mara said I lose my panties around you."

I chuckle. "I'll need to investigate."

"Investigate away, Z."

Damn, she's hard to resist. This woman has become an addiction. She's never far from my thoughts anymore. I can pick up girls anywhere. At Crystal Ball. At the clubhouse. Hell, the damn gas station. But now, I crave being inside Lilly in a way I've never wanted anyone else.

The fact that I don't get to see her every day is frustrating as fuck.

"I'm glad you showed up tonight," she says, a whole lot more serious than the teasing tone she'd used a minute ago.

"Can't seem to stay away from you."

"You didn't want to celebrate your friend's engagement?" A hint of teasing returns.

"Been celebrating it all week. It's *all* the girls have been talking about. And we've been making the obvious ball-and-chain jokes as often as possible to Rock."

She snorts. "That's terrible."

"Nah, he knows we're just fucking with him." At least I am. Teller seemed to take the news hard. Lots of changes coming.

"You're not a little jealous?"

Truth? Yeah, maybe. Not because I'm hot for Hope or

anything. Nope, the woman sitting next to me has put all sorts of things I thought I'd never consider in my head lately. "She's probably the best thing that's ever happened to him. Except meeting me, of course."

"Oh, yes, of course."

Shit, I love the way she's not afraid banter with me. Most girls act like they're either scared of me or they assume I want their lips around my cock and nothing else. Which, I won't lie, is often true.

Not with Lilly.

There's a little activity up at the clubhouse. Mild for a weekend night, really. I tuck her car into the garage—so no one messes with it and so she doesn't skip out on me too early.

She waits for me to open her door and takes my hand. "Need me to carry you?" I ask as she carefully steps over the gravel driveway.

"I'm fine. It's just dark and I'm not used to these shoes."

Call me a caveman, but I can't resist the urge to sweep her into my arms.

"Z, what are you doing?" She laughs and slaps my shoulder. "I'm capable of walking."

I charge up the front steps and set her down inside. Ravage and Stash are getting high in the living room and heckle us instantly.

"Wedding fever catch on?" Rav hollers.

"Shut it." I flip him off and he falls sideways into a girl's lap, laughing like an idiot.

I gesture toward the kitchen. "You hungry?"

Her lips curl into a seductive smirk I know all too well. "I didn't come up here for dinner, Z."

That voice of hers. Seduces me the same as her body. I step closer and brush my lips against her ear. "No? What'd you come here for, then?"

She presses her body hard against mine and leans up to whisper in my ear. "That big, hard dick you're packing."

"You're a dirty girl tonight."

Her gaze stays steady on mine as she backs away. "You like it."

"I fucking love it." Not ready for this to end. I cock my head and bite my lip. "What exactly do you want me to do with my big, hard dick?"

She hooks her fingers in my waistband and tugs. "Anything you want."

"That's a dangerous game, Lilly."

Lilly's fun. Giving in bed. Game for anything. But there's a certain peace or stillness I've only ever felt when I'm deep inside her. Our bodies may be a frenzy of desire and demand. But everything else inside me calms. At times I've felt it's the same for her. That's when I get the real Lilly. Not the one who keeps me at arm's length. The one who's a little fragile under all the flirting.

"Are you two gonna fuck right there?" Ravage shouts, breaking our spell. "At least move closer so there's no glare from the outside lights."

Shaking my head, and ignoring my dickhead brothers, I flip Rav off and take Lilly's hand, dragging her toward the staircase. No surprise, Rock and Hope are nowhere to be seen. Neither are Wrath and Trinity. Probably better that way. I'm not sure Lilly would be this bold in front of her friends.

Two muffler bunnies I recognize are waiting outside Teller's door. I can't tell if they're coming or going and I don't bother to ask. One cocks her head and studies Lilly. Feeling protective, I wrap my arm around Lilly's waist and stare the girl down until she turns her head.

Lilly's not up for grabs. She's not visiting to fuck a patch-holder. She's won't leave my bed in a few hours and stumble next door into another brother's room in some deranged biker bed bingo game she's playing with the other bunnies.

She's mine and mine alone.

Lilly

My heart beats faster as Z unlocks his door. Inside the room, he flips on the lights. There's no time to explore his space. He slides his hands over my cheeks, pulling all of my focus to his face. To his dark-as-the-night-sky eyes. I open my mouth to say something, but he silences me with a kiss. Searing with intensity and unlike any other kiss.

This man is some sort of sex magician, I swear. He presses his body into mine, gently steering us toward his bed. My thoughts and breath are stolen as his hands and mouth roam my body. For such a big man, he's quite adept at unbuttoning my blouse without ripping the delicate fabric. He even goes right for the side zipper of my skirt without hesitation.

"Were you studying my clothes?" I ask as the material pools at my feet.

Z likes to play the pretty boy-biker, but he's a clever man. He knows exactly what I mean. One corner of his mouth slides up. "I'm always searching for ways to strip you out of your clothes."

"I'd like to return the favor." I slide my hands up under his T-shirt, eager to see every magnificent inch of him.

"You in a hurry to get this over with, pretty girl?"

"Hell no. I like you naked."

Grinning, he steps back and shrugs off his cut, neatly draping it over a chair next to his closet. Slowly, he lifts his sweatshirt and I swear my fingertips tingle at the prospect of touching his skin. Without realizing it, I take a few steps closer. His gaze roams over my body again.

All night, he's been friendly, affectionate even. Now he's ferocious as he prowls closer. I retreat and he reaches out, grabbing my hip. "Where are you going?" His gaze drops to my breasts and he licks his lips. "I never get over how pretty you are," he whispers.

"Thank you." The compliment combined with the hungry expression on his face sends desire blazing through me.

He drops to his knees but keeps a firm grip on my hips. Holding me in place. I thread my fingers through all his thick black hair and marvel at the softness. "Mmm." He hooks an arm around one leg and nuzzles his face between my thighs. "Keep doing that."

"What?" I run my fingers through his hair again and he rumble-groans with pleasure. "This?"

"Yeah."

My knees go weak when he teases his finger over the thin material of my panties. A moan passes my lips and my head drops back as he slowly increases the pressure. He's gentle and slow, taking his time to make sure I'm more than ready for the night ahead.

I shudder and can barely stand up straight, but I also can't take my eyes off him as he leans in closer to press his lips against the thin, soaked fabric separating his mouth from my pussy. His powerful shoulders and back muscles roll and flex as he hooks his fingers into the elastic at my hips and slowly drags the underwear down my legs.

A bit of his control seems to snap and he forgets all about my panties, leaving them around my ankles. His strong fingers dig into my ass, drawing me closer. "Fuckin' love your pussy," he murmurs before diving in and kissing my most sensitive spot.

I gasp and curl my fingers into his shoulders, hanging on for dear life. Z's done with the gentle exploration. He runs his tongue through my slit, stopping to tease my clit before starting over. Slow, burning pleasure builds inside me. This won't be a quick burst of an orgasm. Z's more talented and focused than that. He likes to draw out the experience until I'm on the verge of crying for his cock.

My thighs tremble and I have to focus on not losing my balance.

He growls, the sound vibrating through me, throwing gasoline on the fire his talented tongue and fingers are already doing to me. He nudges me backward until I have no choice but to lie down.

"Much better," he rasps, placing my feet on the edge of the mattress the way he wants.

"Z," I whisper.

He grasps my ass and runs his tongue around my clit.

"Oh, fuck." My back arches. The words on my tongue evaporate under his sensual assault.

"Hmm?" he hums, prompting me to speak.

I open my eyes and stare. Good God, I'm the luckiest bitch on the planet. The sexiest man I've ever known has his face buried in my pussy, staring up at me, waiting for me to speak.

The devious expression on he's wearing says he's enjoying every moment. When I don't get the words out right away, he slides a finger inside me, further scrambling my brain.

"Fuck, I really want your cock."

"This not doing it for you, pretty girl?" I can hear the damn smirk in his voice as he lazily presses his finger in and out of me. His tongue slides over my clit again and my legs tremble.

Overwhelmed, I press my palms to my face. "No, fuck. Yes, so good." I can't arrange my words. Finally, I give up and allow the pleasure to consume me.

Zero

Lilly's such a firecracker. Real, raw, and honest in all her emotions. She's beautiful to watch as she comes undone. Every damn time.

When she's limp and lifeless, drained of energy from the orgasms I coaxed from her body, I sit back.

Slowly, she recovers and raises herself on one elbow. "What are you still doing down there?"

"Admiring my work."

She laughs and reaches for one of my pillows, tossing it at my head. I grab it out of her hands and pounce on her, caging her underneath me. Still smiling, she loops her arms around my neck. "You're amazing."

"Why, thank you." I lean down to kiss her and she tightens her hold on me.

Quick and greedy, she wraps her legs around my waist and slides her hands down my back. I press my lips to her forehead. "Eager, pretty girl?"

"Yes." Her fingers continue to explore my body, and, more specifically, my jeans. "Let's get these off."

"Want some cock, huh?"

"No, I want *your* cock."

Her lips stay parted, as if she plans to say something else, and then she glances away.

I'll ask her later. Right now, I'm ready to explode. Taking some of my weight off her, I undo my jeans. She helps me push them off most of the way while I grab a condom and smooth it on.

"Oh, good. God, come here," she whispers, cupping my cheeks and pulling me closer. I press my lips to hers, slowly taking my time. We fall into a rhythm, sucking, licking, nipping at each other. Each time I bump my cock against her clit, she moans into my mouth and I swear I could do just this for the rest of the damn night.

I thrust against her again and she lifts her hips. That little tilt allows me to push inside and I groan. Fuck, she's amazing. I break our kiss and stare into her eyes. "Good?"

She wiggles under me and I bite my lip. "Give me a second to adjust," she whispers. "Angus is the perfect name for you. You're hung like a bull."

"Jesus Christ." I burst out laughing, the movement helping me slide in even more. She moans and arches her back, shoving her tits in my face. I capture one nipple between my lips, sucking hard. My cock slides in a few more inches and her walls tighten around me.

I squeeze my eyes shut, no longer laughing. No, I want to savor this. I love women of all variety. Love pussy, but dammit, everything about Lilly is fucking exceptional.

I stare into her eyes again as I fall into a quick, relentless pace, grinding against her clit with each thrust. "How's that?" I rasp.

"Fucking amazing. Harder."

God, I love her filthy mouth.

Love that dark pink flush racing over her chest and up her neck too. "You gonna come again, Lilly? Think you have it in you?"

She plants her feet on the mattress and raises her hips. "Oh, I have it in me all right."

Again, I laugh, slowing down my frantic thrusts, and drop my forehead to hers. "I love—fucking you."

What the fuck did I almost say?

If she noticed, she doesn't show it. Her head's thrown back, eyes closed, nails digging into my shoulder. I know that look.

"That's it, pretty girl. Come nice and hard on my dick."

"Oh." Her lips part and a low moan escapes. Her hips buck and she tightens all around me. I'd love to wait until I know for sure she's finished, but that look on her face does me in.

I give a few final, brutal thrusts before joining her, the rush of orgasm blazing through me. Hotter and more intense than usual.

"Fuck." I throw myself down next to her, my sweaty back hitting the comforter. The air instantly cools my overheated skin. She turns, draping one arm over my chest and one leg over mine. I love that she's a cuddler. I curl an arm around her, idly playing with her hair.

"Z," she whispers.

"Hmm?"

"You mind if I take a shower?"

"Fuck no." I smirk at her. "I'll even join you."

Her eyes sparkle. Looks like my firecracker's feeling frisky again. "Good, because I didn't get a chance to suck your cock."

"Damn, you're right."

Shaking with laughter, she presses her forehead against my chest and I wrap both arms around her.

Not ready to let go.

Lilly

Freshly showered and fucked, we stumble out of his bathroom and into the bedroom. At the foot of the bed, he rips the towel off me and tosses it in the direction of the door.

"Now I'm naked."

"That's the point."

I reach out and rip his towel off. He holds out his arms, proudly showing off his body. "I got nothing to hide, baby."

"Don't I know it." I glance at the bed. "Do you have a shirt or something?"

He struts over to the dresser and I drool over his tight ass and hard, muscled legs. After finding a pair of shorts for himself, he pulls out a T-shirt and shuts the drawer.

He holds out the shirt, but as I reach for it, he yanks his arm back. "You planning to stick around until morning at least?" His dimples flash. While his tone seems flippant, there's something darker lurking under the question. Maybe he's testing the waters to see how I'll respond?

"If you want me to." I reach for the shirt again and this time he releases it.

He flips the overhead light off and has me crawl into the bed first.

"Yeah, I want you to stay." He settles against the pillows and tucks one arm behind his head. "Definitely don't want you driving all the way back to Lake George in the middle of the night."

Oh, so it's a safety thing. I almost open my mouth to challenge him and say that, then decide not to bother. Why ruin a good thing? "You have any idea how early I'm up and driving into work just to avoid the traffic jam at the Twin Bridges?"

He turns ever-so-slightly. "You should move closer."

Closer to him or closer to work?

"I like my place. Plus, my parents and brother are close by."

He shrugs. "You plan to look for another job?"

"No, I love my job. When they're not in session, I get to take long stretches of time off or work from home, so it all evens out."

I glance over and his eyes are shut. "Sorry, I didn't mean to bore you."

"You're not. I love listening to your voice."

"Because it's putting you to sleep?"

He reaches over and grabs my hand, settling it on his crotch, all without opening his eyes. "No, because it gets my dick hard."

I squeeze him gently through his shorts and he groans. "You definitely need to stay the night. I need to fuck you again in the morning."

Impulsively, I lean in and kiss his cheek. "Whoever wakes up first can get to work on the other."

"Be prepared to wake up with my face in your pussy."

Laughing, I turn over and tuck my arm under the pillow. Behind me, I feel him shift. It's dark and surprisingly quiet in the clubhouse, but I sense him hesitating or holding his breath or something. "What's wrong?" I mutter.

"Nothing."

He shifts again, the warm, solid wall of his body snuggling up behind me. His heavy arm drapes over my waist and he pulls me against his body. "You make a nice pillow," he murmurs, pressing a kiss to my temple.

Who would have ever suspected this giant biker with the impish smile was such a snuggler? I run my hand over his arm and curl into his body, before drifting to sleep.

Z makes good on his promise and wakes me up at least two more times during the night. The last time, I don't even bother to put his shirt back on.

Way, way too early the jingle-jangle of my most obnoxious ring tone wakes me. Worried it will wake Z, I scurry around the room to find my phone and answer it.

There are about a dozen texts from Sophie. Jesus, it's not even eight o'clock.

Sophie: Ben got called into work. Can you take me to get my car?

Shit.

I glance at Z and then at the phone. I really don't want to leave him.

Which is exactly why I should.

Me: Give me an hour.

Wake Z, or just leave? I'm not sure I can handle the thorny morning after talk. Plus, if I stay much longer, I'll run into Hope and that will probably be awkward as hell.

As I tiptoe down the clubhouse stairs, I realize there's something much more awkward than running into my friend.

Running into Wrath.

"Morning, Lilly." He greets me with a big grin on his scary face. His gaze shoots upstairs. "Didn't want to do the awkward morning talk?"

"No." I stop to slip on my shoes. "I have to get home. Something came up."

"Sure, sure." He motions to the front door, as if saying I'm free to make my escape. I barely restrain myself from flipping him off. How does Hope stand him?

Outside, the burly redhead is tinkering with one of the bikes in the garage. My car's blocked.

I bet Z did that on purpose.

"Uh, hi." I wave to get his attention. "Murphy, right?"

"Yeah." He lifts his chin when he sees me. "Hey."

I point at my car. "I need to get out."

He glances around. "Give me a minute."

My phone goes off again.

Sophie.

"All right already."

"Something wrong?" Murphy asks.

"Just my friend needs me to take her somewhere and she's damn impatient."

He kicks over the bike and pulls it out of the garage, then moves one of the other cars.

"Thank you!" I hurry over to my car and ease my way out between all the other vehicles.

Sophie owes me big time.

4

———————————

WEDDING FEVER

This short story was originally published in
Between Embers (Lost Kings MC #5.5)

Lilly

"DON'T BE MAD, but I'm driving behind a really pretty girl."

"What?" I ask.

Z repeats the bizarre statement.

"Did you really call me to tell me you're out picking up chicks on my best friend's wedding day?"

His laughter comes through the line, low and rich. If he were in front of me, I'd kick him.

"I'm driving behind *you.*"

"Oh." My gaze flicks to the rearview mirror, but all I see is a big, black SUV. "Figures that's what you're driving. It looks like an undercover FBI vehicle."

He chuckles again and this time his laughter melts me like butter. "It's Rock's."

"What are you doing?"

"I needed to run an errand for him. What are *you* doing? I thought you stayed with Hope and Trin last night?"

"I did." Z had been pretty annoyed I didn't sneak out and come stay with *him*. But for once in my life, I chose girlfriends over dick. I didn't regret it either. "I needed to run out for a topcoat."

"What?"

"Nail polish. For the bride."

"Ohhhkay."

"Shut up."

"Let me get ahead of you so I can open the gate."

I pull my car slightly to the right and he zips around me, flipping his blinker on and turning onto what barely looks like a road. It's a good thing he found me because I'm not sure I would have remembered to turn here.

It isn't the first time I've wondered about all the secrecy surrounding the Lost Kings MC. Z's usually tight-lipped about anything related to the club. Not that I ask a lot of questions. Or that we do a lot of talking.

But now that one of my best friends is marrying into the club, I'm curious. Hope is a lawyer. And based on the multiple warnings my brother has given me to stay away from Z, the Lost Kings are criminals.

Alexander—what I call my brother when he's busy lecturing me on how to live my life because it annoys him when I use his full name—doesn't understand that Rock treats Hope like a fucking queen. It's hard not to be intrigued.

I don't want that. I don't need a man in my life permanently. Just in my bed from time to time. Z has been all too willing to offer those services on what's becoming a regular basis.

I park a little way down the driveway—in case I want to leave early. Z parks next to me and opens my car door before I have a chance to grab my bag and purse.

"Why'd you park all the way down here?"

"I didn't want to get blocked in if I need to run out again."

He gives me a skeptical look, as if he's not buying my bullshit. Before I explain further, he extends his hand and, I swear to the big stone Buddha statue at the bottom of the hill, I want to swoon. And I'm not a swooner.

A few seconds later, I want to do something else.

Z shuts my door, then presses me up against it with his big, bulky body. "You have any idea what it did to me last night? Having you under the same roof, but not being able to touch you?"

The minute his body brushes against mine, any self-restraint I'd been holding on to flies away in the sweet autumn breeze.

Zero

Lilly's beautiful eyes widen but her body melts against mine. "Tell me," she says in the same husky tone she uses after we fuck.

Rock expressed a strong preference that I not bother the girls last night. Since he's the groom, and my president, I didn't.

"It made me crazy." That's not a lie, either. It's been way too long since I've had Lilly. Knowing she was here last night under the same roof, and I couldn't have her, made me half-crazed with lust.

Tonight's another story.

The happy couple will be enjoying their wedded bliss, and I'll be enjoying Lilly.

"I forgot the stuff I ran out to get. Fuck," she mutters, pushing away from me and opening the door.

Inside, I'm groaning. The way her luscious mouth spits out the word *fuck* is incredibly hot. Reminds me of the way she says it when she's riding my dick.

I need to make that happen again.

Soon.

Like right now. Because having Lilly bent over in front of me while she stretches across the front seat to grab her tiny plastic bag seriously tests my restraint. It's a battle with my inner horndog not to fit my hands over her perfectly curved hips, yank her pants down, and slam into her.

I'm hard just picturing it.

She backs out of the car, bumping right into my groin,

and pure instinct makes me put my hands on her hips. "Sorry," she says, straightening up.

My hands stay where they are. I close the car door and this time press her front to the car, fitting myself against her back. Lifting her thick, heavy hair up, I push it over one shoulder. My lips find her neck and my hips grind against her ass—just enough to tease her.

"Z, what are you doing?" She can barely get the words out.

"Preview of what's going down later."

"Oh, really?" she says in her teasing way. "I thought weddings were great for meeting chicks."

Slowly, I inch back and turn her to face me. "You're the only chick I want. And we've already met. Several times."

She snorts, and I fit my fingers under her chin, lifting her head so she meets my eyes. "I'm not feeding you bullshit, Lilly."

Doesn't she get it by now?

"What if I wasn't in the wedding party?"

"Then you would've been my plus one."

She drops a little bit of her prickly wall and leans into me, brushing a soft kiss on my cheek. Before she pulls away, I lift my hands to either side of her head, holding her still so I can kiss her deeper, really taking my time to remind her of all the ways our bodies fit perfectly together.

A soft moan flows out of her mouth into mine and her hands go to my waistband, yanking me closer.

"Something to think about," I say when we part.

"I'll be thinking about it," she whispers.

Instead of pushing her into the woods, tearing off her clothes, and fucking her up against a tree, I take Lilly's hand and lead her up the driveway.

There's a wedding to get ready for.

Inside the clubhouse, I reluctantly let go of Lilly's hand. After yanking her to me for one last kiss. "See you in a bit."

Her cheeks turn a bit pink, which is cute on Lilly. Few things embarrass her.

Like a lovesick pup, I watch her until she stops at Trinity's door.

Sparky and Stash are hanging out in the living room, rolling joints. "Party favors," Sparky says, then falls over into a fit of giggles.

"Good to see you're ready for the wedding," I bite out. They ignore my sarcasm and keep rolling.

"Idiots," I mutter.

"I heard that," Sparky yells as I run up the stairs. Ignoring the stoner twins, I stride down the hallway and knock on Rock's door. Well, after tonight, it won't be his room anymore. He and Hope are finally moving into their house. If I were sentimental, I might have some words about that.

Okay, I'm a little sentimental. It's the end of an era.

Am I jealous?

Maybe.

Rock's standing in front of his dresser fixing the knot in his tie. I flick my gaze at Wrath, positive it's killing him not to poke fun at our best friend for the suit and tie. His mouth turns up in a grin. Twenty bucks says he's already ribbed Rock about the suit.

"Ready?" I ask Rock.

"Fuck yes." His eyes meet mine, and I sense the briefest hesitation in them. "She's still here, right?"

"Oh, Christ," Wrath mutters. "Cinderella isn't going anywhere."

"Nah, I made sure I locked the front gate after me," I add helpfully.

"Thanks, asshole," Rock growls.

Satisfied or fed up with the tie, Rock drops his hands and turns away from the mirror. "What'd Loco want?"

"Oh." Yeah, meeting up with Lilly had wiped my brain clean of the whole reason I went out in the first place. I yank an envelope out of my pocket and hand it to Rock. "Wedding present. I think he was insulted he didn't get an invite."

"For fuck's sake," he curses under his breath, grabbing the envelope and setting it on the dresser without opening it. "With the crews we have coming in, that's all we would have needed."

Imagining that scenario makes me laugh and Rock glares at me. "What? Come on, that'd be some funny shit."

"More like Loco would be trying to make deals with everyone behind our backs," Wrath says.

Rock doesn't even turn around. "Exactly."

"He's already got something set up with Sway."

"Yeah, can you imagine him trying to work a deal with

Stump?" Wrath's mouth curls into a smirk. "That old bastard would probably shoot Loco." He chuckles as if he's reconsidering inviting Loco up.

"I don't want anything going wrong today." Rock's so damn tense. When he's not looking, I make a *what the fuck* face at Wrath.

"Hope imposed a no-sex-before-the-wedding thing on him," Wrath explains.

Rock glares at him. "Shut up."

Well, that explains it. I take a more serious look at my best friend. I've known Rock since we were teenagers. Was there for his first shitshow of a marriage.

"You did good, Prez. She's a keeper," I say to reassure him. Just in case.

He responds with a brief smile. "Don't I know it."

The three of us have been friends for a long damn time. Before the club. And we love to joke around, razz each other, and generally act like obnoxious fucks. But Rock turns to both of us with a serious expression. "Thank you for everything. I know I'm throwing a lot on both of you today—"

Wrath isn't one for all the feel-good shit. "Anything you need. You know that, brother."

Rock's phone buzzes. Thank fuck. For a second, I thought we were all going to kick back and pluck our eyebrows together.

"Shit," Rock grumbles, looking at his phone. "It's Damon. Can you go meet them down the road and show them the way here?"

Eager to get out of here, I'm saying yes before he even finishes the sentence. Wrath stands to join me, but I stop him. "I got it, bro."

He flips me off. Happy to have something useful to do, I hustle out the door.

Lilly

"I'm back," I call out as I enter Trinity's room, waving the bottle of topcoat in the air.

"Thank God," Trinity says, rushing over to take the bottle out of my hand.

No one asks why I took so damn long. Good thing, because I'm too busy reliving my moments with Z. He seemed different somehow today. Do guys get fluttery romantic feelings at weddings the way some women do?

Guys like Z? Doubt it.

I certainly don't.

I'm thrilled for Hope, but I'm not standing here, mentally picking out flowers and designing a wedding dress.

While Trinity paints Hope's nails, I duck into the bathroom to slip into my bridesmaid dress. Hope's been a fun, unfussy bride. She let us pick out whatever we wanted, didn't expect elaborate parties, or any other bridezilla nonsense. The wedding really is about the two of them and their love for each other. Even someone as jaded as I am finds it sweet.

Once I've secured my boobs and zipped my dress, I step out in time to watch Trinity fix Hope's hair.

We indulge in a lot of pre-wedding banter until it's time for Z to come collect us.

Other than trading in his jeans for a pair of gray cargo pants, he looks the same as always.

"You didn't dress up for the wedding?" I tease as I follow the girls outside.

"Sure I did." He grins, pointing to his pants and flashing dimples.

Z's drives Hope, Trinity, and me to the wedding site. Heidi's with Murphy. Teller gets Mara. When Hope first explained the wedding was happening at the clubhouse, I thought she was nuts. But as we maneuver through the woods in the UTV, I understand why. It's beautiful.

I can't imagine the trouble Trinity must have gone to setting this up. Guilt simmers over me for not being a better bridesmaid.

We park and Z helps Hope out. She and Rock meet and, well, they're in their own little world. Wrath meets Trinity and asks where Heidi and Murphy are. Somehow, we lost them along the way.

Z walks up and offers me his hand. "Hey, pretty girl." His low, smooth voice does all sort of inappropriate things to my insides.

My voice fails me, and I realize I'm staring at him like an idiot. Finally, I reach out and take his hand and a jolt of awareness heats my body.

He sort of dips his head, almost like a shy gesture. Z's

anything but shy, so I'm intrigued. "You're…that color's beautiful on you. You look amazing."

His words come out so serious that, again, I'm at a loss for words.

"Were you guys drinking this morning?" he asks as we join the others.

"No. Why?"

"You seem off." He leans in close to whisper in my ear, "And because I need you fully sober for all the things I plan to do to you when this is over."

Our eyes meet and he winks.

He takes his place across the aisle from me, leaning over to say something in Wrath's ear. The big blond chuckles softly and nods.

Zero

"Twenty dollars says they're fucking before this thing's over," I say to Wrath in a low voice when I join him on Rock's side of the aisle.

He shakes with laughter and nods but doesn't respond. He's too fixated on Trinity. Probably thinking about what kind of wedding she'll arrange for them.

My gaze drifts to Lilly. Fuck, she ripped the air right out of my lungs when I saw her this morning. She's prickly, though. Probably have to *trick* her into marrying me.

The ceremony's over quick. Boxes of butterflies are passed around and everyone releases them into the air.

I've really had my fill of all this girly shit. But based on what I've seen some of my cousins go through with their wives, I suppose it could have been a lot worse. Rock's a lucky bastard.

Would Lilly be some crazed bride, trying to micro-manage everything down to my underwear? Or would she be happy with something simple like this?

I doubt I'll ever know.

Shit. In the last few months, I've watched the two people in the world closest to me voluntarily settle down. It leaves me coming up with a lot of stupid ideas.

Unfortunately, the only girl on my mind these days is Lilly. Even though she'll dodge me for weeks at a time, I still can't get enough of her. The amount of fucks I should give that I have to chase after her are hard to come up with.

Lilly

"You think about gettin' married?" Z asks as he watches Rock feed Hope a bite of cake.

The wedding was beautiful. Food has been amazing. Poor Trinity's been running around all night.

And Z's asking me if I think about marriage? "God, no," I finally answer.

"Never?"

A catch in his voice makes me turn my head. *"You* do?"

"Yeah," he states matter-of-factly.

"Why?"

He stares at me as if a flock of butterflies just flew out of my mouth instead of a one-word question. "Same reason anyone does." He nods at Rock and Hope, who are so immersed in each other it almost feels like an invasion of privacy to watch them.

"I don't think everyone who gets married has what they have," I say as I turn back toward Z.

"No. Probably not."

While I admire my friend for sticking by her man while he went through some trouble this summer, I know for a fact I couldn't do it. Visit Z in jail? No way. It would break me. Not to mention how horrified my family would be. It's not like I can't guess that Z's motorcycle club is more than a club. That they're into some shady stuff. Maybe Hope managed to convince herself of her husband's innocence, but since meeting Z, I've heard enough stories about the Lost Kings MC to know that they're anything but innocent. While Z's hot, great in bed, and super sweet, he's not marriage material.

I don't think explaining any of that at his best friend's wedding is the polite thing to do, so I force a smile instead.

Besides, I wasn't lying. The last thing I want to do is get married. Let any man think he owns me. And a guy like Z would definitely be the *I-own-you* caveman-type of husband.

Fuck that.

"Marriage is for suckers," the guy across from us says, slurring each word. He has the nerve to jab a ham-sized finger in the air at me. "She's hot now, but give her ten years. She'll be fat and do nothing but bitch at ya."

Z leans over the table, grabbing the guy by his shirt. "Watch your fuckin' mouth, asshole." He growls a few more warnings, so low I can't hear them. The guy ends up shuffling away after flipping Z off.

"Sorry," he mutters as he sits back down.

"One of your brothers?" It's hard to keep the sarcasm out of my voice.

"Sort of. He's from another charter and he's a dick. No one here would ever think something like that, let alone say it."

It's true. None of the guys I've met before have ever been rude. Slightly terrifying, yes. Rude, no.

Trinity breezes by and drops into the chair next to me. "Are you having fun?" she asks breathlessly.

"Are *you*? You've been running non-stop all day."

She waves off my concern. "I'm done for the night."

"Sure you are," I tease.

Trinity's boyfriend…no there's nothing *boy* about him. Trinity's *man* lumbers over, settling a hand on her shoulder. They stare at each other with complete adoration for a few seconds, before he lifts his chin at Z.

The two guys do this unspoken conversation thing that's actually fascinating to watch. Next thing I know, Z's sliding his chair back.

"I need to take care of something. You okay?"

"Sure, as long as that guy doesn't come back."

Z's gaze searches the tent. "If anyone bothers you"—he points out two guys with Lost Kings MC cuts on—"let Dex or Ravage know." He shifts and I follow his line of sight. "You know Murphy and Teller. They'll look out for you, too."

"Uh, okay."

"I'll take care of her, Z. Go ahead," Trinity says. She pokes Wrath in the side. "Go do what you need to so you can hurry back." He flashes a smile so warm he almost doesn't look so scary. After they're gone, she raises an eyebrow at me. "Someone bother you?"

"Not really." I don't want to seem like I'm complaining. I've dealt with plenty of rude, drunk men in my life. I can handle it. "So, you really went with a monarch theme," I tease, nodding at the table at the head of the room where the bride and groom are.

Tittering laughter bubbles out of her. "Yeah. The whole king and queen thing. That's what we do here."

A young woman slides into the seat across from us. "Hey," she greets.

Trinity flashes a tight smile at the girl. "How's it going, Sasha?"

"This is really something."

"Is it your first LOKI wedding?"

"Yes." The girl swings her vacant gaze my way. "Whose old lady are you?"

"Uh," I glance at Trinity unsure how to answer the

question. From spending time with Z and listening to Hope, I know what an old lady is. Well, I know enough to know that's not what I am to Z.

"She's with our VP," Trinity answers for me.

"Oh."

"Who are you with?" I ask to be friendly.

She lifts a lazy finger, pointing across the room at a cluster of guys with cuts claiming a different territory than Z's. "Crazyhorse. I ain't his old lady, though. Well—" she giggles. "I am at club events. His wife's one-hundred percent citizen."

I'm not sure how to respond to that. I glance at Trinity, who's staring daggers at the girl. Before she responds, someone calls her away. "I'll be right back."

Leaning forward, I catch Sasha's attention. "Forgive me, but what did you mean about citizen?" I ask, because, hell, I'm curious.

"Oh. You know. She's like his wife outside the club. Like, legal wife. Raises his kids, takes care of the house. But when he's with me, it's all just fun, you know?"

"And she knows about you?"

She gives me a sly grin. "I'm sure she does."

"And you're okay just being his piece of ass?"

She snorts, not insulted—not that I care if she is. "Yeah. I get to do the fun stuff with him. All bikers are like that. They all date you know, like, girls *my* age," she says, as if she wants to really make sure I understand that I'm an old hag or something.

"That's fascinating." She doesn't even blink at the caustic tone of my voice.

"So you're new to the life, then? Like her?" She jerks her thumb in Hope's direction. "She's so fucking stuck-up."

This chick realizes I was in the wedding, right? "She's actually one of my best friends. And she's as far from stuck-up as a person can get."

"Oh." Her lips quiver into a smile. "Sorry. I haven't, uh really talked to her much."

"Then maybe you shouldn't run your mouth about stuff you know nothing about?"

"Whatever." She stands and storms off.

I guess I got a pretty good dose of reality tonight. If I ever thought about Z and I being something more permanent—which I don't—I'd have to put up with him having club girls on the side while I sit home, pretending I didn't know what he was up to.

Double fuck that.

What we have is perfect. What we have is all we'll ever be.

I don't recognize the guys at the table next to us. But they're wearing Lost Kings MC cuts like Z's. Their bottom rockers claim downstate New York as their territory. One loud drunk catches my attention. He aims his glare at Murphy, who's up front talking to Rock. "That ginger fuck is so far up her ass, it ain't even funny. You believe none of them were fuckin' her while he was inside?"

A round of drunk noises of disbelief go around the

table. Are they talking about Hope? I lean back in my chair a little further, straining to catch more of their conversation without appearing obvious.

"Sorry," Trinity says, setting her hand on my shoulder and dropping into the chair next to me.

My face must betray the eavesdropping I was attempting. "Everything okay?" she asks.

"Oh, yeah. Who are those guys? The loud one?" I tip my head toward the downstate table.

"That's the president of our downstate charter." Her eyes narrow as she studies my face. "He didn't bother you, did he?"

"No. Nothing like that."

"Okay. Z should be back any second."

Right after she says it, her man strides back into the tent. He takes a seat next to her and pulls her into his lap.

Now, where is Z?

As if my body's aware of his every movement, my gaze lands on him coming in the back of the tent.

He searches the crowd and when his eyes meet mine, his mouth curves into a wide smile.

It really sucks that he's so fucking gorgeous, he makes my knees weak every time he flashes his dimples my way.

Zero

"What the fuck does Stump want?" I grumble at Wrath once we're away from the wedding tent.

"How the fuck should I know?" he grumbles right back. "I have my own things to take care of tonight."

I slap his arm with the back of my hand. "Care to share?"

"No."

The clubhouse will be too packed to discuss business. We head down to the stone amphitheater where the wedding was held. Any meetings we needed to have with visiting MCs tonight would happen out here. Wrath and Murphy have the honor of dealing with the Wolf Knight sit-down. Wrath and I get to deal with the Devil Demon's president, Stump.

Stump's actually not a bad guy. He's old as fuck, though. His son, Chaser, should really be running things by now, but Stump isn't giving up control of his club any time soon. Chaser is the VP and he's sitting in on this meeting as well.

"Can't believe your prez went through with that," Stump says after we get greetings out of the way.

Like the half-caveman he is, Wrath grunts. "She's a good girl."

"Where we at on my supply?" Stump asks.

Wrath answers that question. "We're still tight. Demand's high. We have certain people aware of our connection, so you might want to look into that."

Stump cocks his head to the side. "Maybe the leak's on your end."

"Unlikely," I answer.

Father and son share a look, but don't comment

further. As if they're already aware there might be a problem in their crew.

Not my business.

To keep the peace, I offer up a small quantity that the club agreed to ahead of time. "Sparky set aside an O for you to take home."

Stump aims a pissed-off biker expression my way. An ounce is way under the quantity the Demons were looking to purchase.

"On the house," Wrath adds. "It's a new strain Sparky cultivated. Slightly higher THC count."

Stump's irritation disappears. Who can be mad about free weed? Especially the quality shit we're known for growing.

"Appreciate that," he says.

Thank fuck for Sparky and his miracle green thumbs. "Just talk to Sparky or Stash before you leave."

"Anything else?" Wrath asks. He's calm and controlled. Only because I know him so well is it obvious that he's itching to get this over with.

While Stump's a decent guy, he's also a talker. Something Wrath doesn't have a whole lot of patience for. Honestly, I don't have much patience for it either since I want to get back to Lilly.

Stump's face pulls into a mask of seriousness. "I have a request."

"Actually, *I* do," Chaser says. "My son, Dylan. He's gonna be at Empire State next semester. I'm—"

"You want us to look out for him?" I ask.

"Kind of. He's a good kid. Not a lot of trouble." He nods at Wrath. "He's been into MMA since—"

"Since his sister pelted him in the ass with her BB gun," Stump interrupts with a laugh. "That's how he got tagged with Target."

"Good road name." I snicker.

Chaser sighs and runs his hand over his chin. "Yeah."

Wrath actually cracks a smile. "The sister's not coming too, is she?"

Stump glares at Wrath for asking about his granddaughter, even though we all know Wrath didn't mean anything by it. "Fuck no. She ain't—"

"Anyway," Chaser says, interrupting his father. "He'd like to train with you." He nods at Wrath.

"He can come into Furious whenever. No problem," Wrath says. He does *not* say anything about having the kid up to the clubhouse.

"He ride?" I ask.

The old man's face pulls down in disgust while Chaser rolls his eyes. "Fuckin' rice burner," Stump spits out.

Next to me, Wrath's choking down his laughter. Obviously, his grandson's choice of bike is killing Stump.

Chaser shrugs. "He bought it with his own money."

"I'll still let him train at Furious," Wrath says, barely keeping the grin off his face.

"We've had trouble with the Viper charter trying to push up from Pennsylvania. Just in case. Want to make sure he's protected."

"He living on campus?" I ask.

Chaser shrugs. "Think so. Haven't ironed it all out yet."

"You got our numbers. Let us know what you need. We'll keep an eye on him." Wrath gives me a look, like he's not interested in babysitting some other club's kid. But we have a long history with the Demons. Helping them out isn't a big hardship and earns us a favor down the road.

Lilly

"Miss me?" Z asks, leaning over the back of my chair. His fingertips brush over my bare shoulder, setting off sparks of desire.

"Actually, yes." Why lie?

He pulls me out of my chair, making Trinity laugh. His hands fit over my hips, yanking me close to dance for a few songs. Every press of his body against mine makes me wish we were alone.

After Hope and Rock make their exit—and Z made it clear he expects me to stay over—I'm ready to rip his clothes off and have my way with him in the woods, if need be.

"You've got a lot of pretty girls here. Sure you want me to stick around?"

He pulls back, and I want shove the words back into my mouth. I'm never so insecure around a guy. Tonight I'm rattled, for lots of reasons.

"Yeah, Lilly. I want you to stick around," he says so seriously my heart thumps.

"Are you drunk?" I ask.

"Not at all," he answers in a tone of voice that's almost grave.

I don't need a whole lot of convincing. Although staying at the clubhouse reminds me an awful lot of sleeping at a frat house, I'm not sure where else we'd go at this hour.

"Heading out?" the big scary blond one asks with a smirk. Z punches him in the arm and he barely reacts, except to laugh.

"Do you need me?" Z asks, dropping the attitude.

"Nah, we're good. I'm going to head back in a few minutes myself."

The glow from the wedding site only carries so far, but Z seems very sure of where he's going. He does take my hand, though. "Sorry, all the UTVs are being used, or I would drive us back."

"It's fine. It's pretty at night." It is, too. Except for the party going on behind us, it's peaceful…tranquil up here. I can see why Z likes it so much.

A couple of guys are in the yard in front of the clubhouse. Z doesn't stop to talk to any of them.

"In a hurry?" I tease.

"Yeah. Don't want you to change your mind."

"Hey." I stop and yank on his hand until he looks at me. "I'm not leaving."

He flashes a quick smile, dimples and all, then leans in until we're so close, I can taste the sweet mint on his breath.

"You want me, pretty girl?"

I lose myself in his clear blue eyes. Endless midnight blue like a cold winter night sky. "I always want you."

He closes the distance and our lips meet. Slow at first. For a rough guy, Z can be awfully gentle when he wants to be. Then his fingers grip my ass, pulling me closer. My mouth opens and he slides his tongue inside, stroking softly.

Someone whistles at us, and he pulls away. I duck my head, not sure why I'm embarrassed. Z doesn't bother answering the catcall. Instead, he leads me into the clubhouse. Except for two guys and a girl in the living room, the downstairs is deserted.

"Give me a second?" Z asks.

I nod, and he pulls me over to the couch. "Hey, Willow." He nods at the girl, and she smiles back.

Jealousy sinks its dirty claws into my skin. Who is she? How do they know each other? Maybe Z senses the change in me. He squeezes my hand and pulls me closer. "Lilly, this is Willow. She tends bar for us down at Crystal Ball. Willow, this is my girl, Lilly." He doesn't look at me or stumble over the words *my girl*.

I don't know how I feel about that. I'm a grown-ass woman. I should be insulted. But I kind of like Z introducing me as his girl.

Willow nods and gives me a warm smile while Z continues introducing me to his brothers, Sparky and Stash.

"Interesting road names, guys."

Sparky grins but doesn't offer a story behind his name.

Niceties over with, Z gets down to business. "Stump's gonna stop by later for—"

Sparky cuts him off with a serene smile and quick, "Got it."

Z nods and takes me upstairs.

Briefly, I wonder which one of the scary guys at the wedding was named Stump and what he's stopping by for.

"You need me to watch the dogs, brother?" Sparky asks with a quick glance at me.

Z grins. "Yeah. You mind?"

"Nope."

Sparky follows us upstairs and when Z opens his door, two pups wriggle out, dancing and pawing at Z's legs.

"Down," he orders them.

"Oh my God, they're so sweet!" I squeal like a little girl. Squatting down, I take a few minutes to pet them. "Hope mentioned the dogs. I didn't realize they were yours." I tilt my head so I can see Z's face.

He shrugs. "They're the club's dogs, but I'm training them."

Sparky lets a short, sharp whistle loose and the pups snap to attention.

"Looks like they answer to him too." I chuckle.

Z's not one of those guys who feels his manhood's been threatened when his dogs listen to someone else. "It's good for them to be used to other people."

They follow Sparky back downstairs. "Don't get them

high," Z shouts after him. Sparky's laughter is the only answer we get.

Fun time's over. Z's face is almost ferocious as he nudges me into his room and shuts the door. He wraps his arms around me, pushing my back against the wall. "Eager much?" I tease.

"Fuck yeah. I don't think you understand what you do to me, Lilly."

Yes I do, because I feel the same way. Z takes my hand and kisses my fingertips. There's something about this big, beautiful, tattooed, dimpled man that makes my heart kick up every damn time he focuses his attention on me. Warmth rushes through my veins. Tingles race up and down my spine. He's the only one who's ever had this effect on me.

His blue eyes bore into mine, shining with lust and need. Need that hits me right between my thighs. My body always reacts this way to Z whether I want it to or not.

Good thing I want it. Want *him*. Bad.

"Do you want me to fuck you, Lilly?" he asks with his serious expression in place.

"Yes." I don't bother hesitating or doing the hard-to-get thing. Z would see right through it anyway.

Tipping my head to the side, I take in his room.

"You've been here before," he reminds me.

Yes, except I'd come in tipsy with him in the middle of the night. We'd gotten off, slept for a few hours, and I took off before sunrise.

He steps back, and lets his gaze roam over my body.

"Is black your favorite color?" I ask, nodding at the bed with its black comforter and sheets. The furniture's all black lacquer too.

His lips quirk up. "And red."

"Aren't your club's colors blue and gray?"

He cocks his head. "You know my club's colors?"

"Well," I hedge, "it's hard not to."

He lifts a hand, tracing a finger over my collarbone and down to the keyhole opening in my dress. "Did you know red was my favorite color?"

"No. It just looks really good on me."

"Fuckin' A it does."

"So, you don't like blue and gray?"

He seems confused by the question. Hell, I'm not even sure why I asked myself.

"It's not about that, Lilly," he says with more seriousness than I think Z's ever spoken anything.

"What's it about?"

"It's not some pretty accessory."

"I think that's pretty clear."

His voice takes on a more solemn tone. "Colors were picked long before I was a member."

"How'd you become a member?"

"How? I don't even know how to answer that."

"Would you answer it?"

He sighs and spreads his hands in front of him. "What do you want to know, Lilly?"

What am I doing? What am I trying to gain from this? "You'll answer my questions?"

He pulls away from me, sitting on the edge of his bed. "I'll answer what I can."

"Can women be members?"

An amused snort bursts out of him. "None have ever asked."

"What about Trinity?"

"She doesn't ride."

"Why not?"

"You'd have to ask her."

"But she's allowed to?"

"Ride? Shit, yeah. She can do whatever she wants."

"The big scary guy would let her?"

My question elicits a soft chuckle out of him. "Please make sure to call him that to his face."

"I'm serious."

"You worried about Trinity?" he asks in his short, clipped way that somehow comes out softer and more happy that I care about Trinity than annoyed by my obnoxious questions. "Trin has a mind of her own. I'm sure if she wanted to ride, she would," he finally says.

"What's the 'property of' thing mean? Seems pretty caveman."

He rolls his eyes before answering. "It's too complicated to explain right now."

"You think I'm too stupid to get it?"

"No. I'm just not sure if you have an open mind. Hope has a patch too, you know."

That's interesting. Maybe I'll ask Hope about it instead, since I don't think I'm going to get anywhere with Z.

"How come Trinity's vest doesn't have the skull and crown?"

This time, I get a lopsided grin. "She ain't a member. Colors are for members."

I'm out of questions.

"You done?" Z asks.

"I reserve the right to ask more questions later."

Reaching out a hand, he crooks his finger at me. "Come here, pretty girl."

I slip my shoes off, leaving them next to his dresser, and make my way to him.

His big hands slide up my legs, up under my dress, until he's gripping my upper thighs. Not hard enough to hurt. Just enough to drive me crazy. "What's with all the questions? You've never been interested in this stuff before."

I can't explain it. Maybe it's from hanging out with all of his brothers tonight. As well as guys from other clubs. Before tonight, I'd only interacted with Hope's now-husband, Rock. I'd seen Trinity's man once or twice. And of course, Z. But tonight was different.

Now, I'm curious.

"I don't know. I realized, hanging out with so many of your brothers, it made me think, I don't know anything about that part of your life."

"You never wanted to."

"So, now I do."

His features turn serious. Serious Z is a little intimidating. "Why?"

"I don't know."

"Is it general curiosity? Or do you want to know *me* better?"

Now, *that's* a loaded question.

Zero

I need to know the answer to my question, but not for the reason she probably thinks. Is she nosy for info about the club so she has some fun stories to tell her friends? Or does she honestly want to know more about *me*?

She seems to think over my question, which doesn't bother me. I like how thoughtful she is about something so important.

"I guess, seeing everyone tonight…I realized your club, it's more than a social thing."

I release my hold on her legs, and she backs up a few steps. "It's a brotherhood."

She shakes her head. "What does that mean?"

"It's about loyalty. We always have each other's backs. No matter what."

"I've only ever felt that way about family."

"They're my family."

"No, my brother—"

"I know what *you* meant. I'm explaining my outlook to you. They *are* my brothers." I tap my fist over my heart so she gets it. "Doesn't matter if we share blood, I'd bleed for anyone of them, and they'd do the same for me." That's the truth, and it's even happened once or twice.

"Does that loyalty extend to the women?"

"Hope and Trinity? Fuck yeah, it does. Teller's sister, Heidi, too."

At the mention of Heidi's name, Lilly's lush mouth turns up in a smile. "She's such a nice kid."

"Yeah, don't let her fool you. She's a little badass. Doesn't need us protecting her as much as you'd think."

Lilly chuckles and I realize I'm having fun talking about this stuff with her. Happy she seems curious and more open-minded than I've given her credit for. I've always appreciated how loyal she is to Hope. Now, the way she seems concerned about Trinity and Heidi—fuck, I like that too. She'd probably rip my balls off for saying it out loud, but Lilly's good ol' lady material.

But I think we've come as far as we can with this conversation for tonight.

"Come back here."

I've been hard for Lilly all day, but the way she reacts to my no-room-for-argument tone, works me up even more. Her breathing kicks up. Short, quick breaths that make her chest rise and fall.

"Turn around."

She hesitates before turning. There's a rush that comes with telling a willful woman like Lilly to do something and watching her struggle between telling me to *fuck off* and doing it that's hot as fuck. My hands find their way to her smooth legs. Tracing my fingers behind her knees and up to the backs of her thighs makes her giggle softly.

"That tickles," she whispers. Laughter turns into a sharp moan when my hands find their way to her ass and squeeze. Perfect.

Reaching up, I drag the zipper of her dress down.

"Take it off."

Her shoulders lift, letting the dress fall to the floor. Gracefully, she leans over and pulls the dress off her foot, tossing it on my desk.

I like the way Lilly holds herself—there's nothing about Lilly I don't like—but I admire her confidence. Straight spine, shoulders back. Her long hair almost reaches the small of her back

Standing, I wrap one arm around her waist and press her tight to me.

I drag my lips over her shoulder. "Admit we're good together, Lilly," I whisper as I kiss my way to her ear.

"So good."

The fact that she didn't bother with a bunch of half-hearted protests or a smartass comeback makes me say something else I wasn't planning on. "You know you're the last thing I think about before I go to sleep? The only face I picture when I close my eyes?" It's so much easier to tell her these things when she's not facing me.

"Me too," she whispers, so low I almost don't hear her. Surprised she'd admit it, I squeeze her a little tighter.

Her head falls forward. But one of her hands sneaks between us, closing around my dick, rubbing the hard length through my pants. I groan, jerking my hips forward.

"You want that?"

"Yes."

"Do you think you deserve it?"

She snorts. "Probably not."

I add my rumbling chuckles to her softer laughter. "Think you can take it?"

"Oh, I know I can."

I move my hand up, cupping her breast, and grazing my thumb over her nipple. Against my body, she shivers.

"Z," she says on a ragged exhale of breath, "don't make me wait."

"Why not? You made me wait. Tortured me last night, knowing you were here and I couldn't have you."

"That's not fair." I can practically hear the pout in her voice.

"No, it wasn't."

Guiding her with my hands on her hips, I turn her to face me. She's tired of me messing with her because she twists her fingers in my hair and pulls me to her for a rough kiss. She crushes my mouth against hers, but that's where I take over. I brush my fingers through her hair, wrapping it tight around my fist and give her a gentle tug. It's enough to make her pause so I can slide my tongue inside her mouth. She breathes a soft moan into me and kisses me back so hard I groan. My lips slide down her jaw to her throat, and she arches her back, pressing herself into me.

I pull away and grip her exploring hands. "Get my dick out." I slip off my shirt and it lands somewhere on the floor. I'm not real worried about it. No, all I can think about is her hands quickly working my pants open, pushing everything down to free my aching dick. A soft hiss of air eases out of me as she takes me in both of her soft hands.

"What do you want?"

Instead of answering, she lowers herself to the floor in front of me. My eyes zero in on her tongue as she runs it over her lips. I'm dying to get inside her, but I'm also having fun teasing her. Gently, I press my hand to her forehead, pushing her back.

"Stay still. I'll let you know when you can have it."

She flicks her eyes up at me in surprise and probably annoyance. I give her a second, and she sits back, waiting for what happens next.

"Open."

The second her lips slide over the head of my cock, my legs hum with pleasure. The sensation travels up my spine. Pleasure leaves me groaning as her warm, wet mouth surrounds me. She swirls her tongue around me, then sucks greedily.

"Good girl."

I get another pissy look for that one, but it only gets me harder.

"Take it all, Lilly."

She takes me right to the back of her throat over and over, never backing off until I hold her head still. "Up."

Lilly

Only slightly annoyed, I kiss my way up Z's body. When I'm standing, he brings his mouth near mine, hovering for a second. I want him to kiss me more than anything.

And he does. He grabs the back of my head and kisses fiercely. I open for him because there's no point denying how much I want him.

I push, but Z's a mountain of man and muscle. Impossible to move.

"What do you want, Lilly?" he asks.

"You."

His lips curve, and there's a hint of arrogance in his eyes that makes me want to smack him. Then he drops his gaze, uses his thumbs to roughly pull my bra down. Frustrated because the material refuses to cooperate, he reaches around and unhooks it, flinging it away. One roughened hand cups my breast the other one dips lower. He holds my gaze as he slides two fingers between my legs. They slip into place easily because I've been ready for him all day.

I'm not prepared for the intense look in his eyes when he spins me around, pushing me onto his bed. The noise in my head goes silent under the weight of his stare. He climbs on the bed after me, kicking his pants and shoes off. "Come here, pretty girl." His raspy voice pulses through my body, filling me with desire.

The crinkle of a wrapper draws my attention from his eyes. I watch him slide into a condom. He eases my knees apart, opening me.

"Yeah, this is what I've been waiting for all fucking day," he says, closing the distance between us. He circles and taps my clit with his cock. Teasing me again. How the hell can he stand it?

"Will you fuck me already?"

My demand finally snaps his iron control, and he pushes into me. Z's a lot to handle, but I love every bit of his thick length inside me.

He groans and halts his movements. "Fuck. You're tight as hell. Miss me?"

"Yes," I whisper because I'm tired of playing hard to get with him. Uncomfortable being so open, I bury my face in his neck. He takes mercy on me and works his hips, each thrust slow, hard, and deliberate.

"Give me your mouth, Lilly."

Shaking my head, I nip at the muscles of his shoulder. "Careful. I might bite back."

I can't help it, though. His massive frame is such a turn-on. I've never been with another man who's such a solid wall of muscle. Who knows how to use all those muscles to please me in every way.

"Lilly," he warns.

I roll my hips up to meet him and he groans. "Fuck. So fucking good," he mutters. His pace slows to a lazy grind and one of his hands grips my chin, turning my face, kissing my lips.

He forces his tongue into my mouth at the same time he drives into my pussy hard and relentless. The dual assault leaves me panting. I raise my legs, wrapping them around his waist.

"Good girl," he praises, slipping a hand under my ass, angling me up even more.

If he wasn't balls deep inside me, I'd smack him for that *good girl* comment. But all I care about are his primal grunts and punishing thrusts.

Every muscle in my body tightens around him, and Z slows, not wanting me to come so quick. But it's too late. I gasp and arch my back and get carried away by a sweeping orgasm.

Zero

Maybe it's the wedding that has her so hot. She claimed not to be the marrying kind, but she's wilder than she's ever been before.

And Lilly is pretty fucking wild.

When she opens her eyes, I slide out of her and urge her onto her hands and knees, thrusting back inside before she's fully ready for me.

"Fuck!" she yells out, and I grunt in agreement. My

arm bands tight around her waist, pulling her against me at the same time as I plow into her. It's hotter. Heat's just pouring off her. Slicker.

So fucking amazing.

Every little flutter, every muscle tightening around my dick, rockets through me. Why aren't we doing this all the time? Why am I waiting for her to figure her shit out instead of telling her how it's going to be? We're fucking amazing together. And if she'd let us, we could be more than fantastic fucking sex.

"Lilly," I groan her name through my release. My entire body stills, tightens, pouring everything I have into her.

I pull in a few shaky breaths before sliding out of her and staggering off the bed. She collapses into a cute little puddle, all plush ass in the air, perfectly thick thighs, unblemished skin and sex-mussed hair.

Something wet hits my foot, and I glance down.

My dick's poking out of the condom, cum leaking everywhere.

"Fuck," I mutter. "Lilly?"

"*Mmm?*" She rolls over and I swear my dick's already getting hard again from just the sight of her fantastic tits.

I point down. "Condom broke. I'm sorry I didn't realize it sooner."

Anger? Horror? Shock? I'm not sure. Maybe a mix of those three emotions flicker over her face. "I'm clean, babe." Oh, I hate like fucking hell admitting this next part. "You're the only one I've—"

She has the nerve to roll her eyes. "I'm supposed to believe that?"

"Believe whatever you want." I stalk into the bathroom and just barely stop myself from slamming the door. I take a few seconds to clean up and calm the fuck down. No one twists me up the way she does. *No one.*

When I emerge, a little more rational, she's sitting in the bed with her knees drawn up, the sheet covering her right to her chin.

"I'm sorry," she says softly. "You're the only...don't worry. I haven't been with anyone else in a long time. We're good."

Any lingering anger disappears, and I pounce on the bed, ripping the sheet away from her and replacing it with my body. "Really?" I ask, drawing the word out until I get her to laugh.

"Yeah, really. Don't be so smug." She reaches out and cups my cheek, her soft fingers brushing against my skin. "I think you've ruined me for any other man."

"Nothing wrong with that." I move in closer for a kiss and she makes this little noise that sounds like either agreement—

Or denial.

***

I could get used to waking up with Lilly next to me.
Even after the broken condom fiasco.

She makes me think about all sorts of things I never considered before meeting her.

But Lilly's a tricky one. I try to talk to her about us moving from fuck buddies to serious couple, she shuts me down.

Every fucking time.

It's annoying. And if she wasn't the hottest fuck I've ever had as well as the smartest chick I've ever spent time with, I would have lost her number long time ago.

Soft scratching at my bedroom door pulls me out of bed. The pups wriggle and dance their way into the room. After being displaced last night, it was a miracle they hadn't howled or scratched at my door all night. "Uncle Sparky take care of you?" I whisper as I bend down to scratch behind their ears. "I owe you two extra cookies."

I throw a quick glance at Lilly—still sound asleep—and slip on a pair of sweats before running the dogs downstairs and outside.

A few guys are still up. Stash and Ravage are busy smoking dope in the living room. Dex is there too, but seems to be halfway sober. Swan's sort of passed out in his lap. I lift my chin at her. "She okay?"

"Yeah," he answers slowly.

"You should have seen the show she put on in the champagne room last night," Ravage says, wiggling his eyebrows for emphasis and earning a scowl from Dex.

Great. Always has to be some complication around here.

"Where's Willow? She go home?" I ask.

Stash raises his eyebrows and points to the basement door. "With Sparky."

"Really?" Man, I can't wait to rib Willow this week at the club.

Stash shrugs, but there's a lingering smirk that makes me want to press him for details.

"Oh my God, why are you guys up at this hour?" Trinity asks from the hallway. I turn and find her dressed to work out, an inexplicable smile stretched across her face.

"What are you doing up so early? Shouldn't you be exhausted from your maid of honor duties? Or from your man?" Ravage asks.

"Watch it," Wrath growls coming up behind her and yanking her against him. He leans down, whispering something in her ear that makes her laugh softly and smack his chest. Without saying anything else, she turns and heads back down the hall.

"Why so grumpy?" I ask.

Wrath grins. "Oh, I ain't grumpy at all."

Intrigued, Ravage and Stash sit up. "What's up, bro?" Ravage asks.

"Nothing. Later."

With those cryptic words, Wrath turns and walks down the hall.

"Something's up with those two," Ravage says.

"Wow. You could be like a detective or something," Stash snarks at him before lighting another joint and inhaling deep.

"Fuck off."

"This has been fun, but I've got a hot, naked chick in my bed."

"Need some help with that?" Stash asks, just to be a dick.

"No, ya fuck," I growl at him.

The two fuckwits have a good laugh. Dex just rolls his eyes. The pups jump up on the couch and settle into the cushions behind Swan.

"Watch them?" I ask.

"Yeah. No problem," Ravage answers.

I take the stairs two at a time and let out a breath when I find Lilly still sound asleep.

Fuck, I like having her here.

I slip into bed next to her and watch as she slowly wakes.

"Morning."

She gives me an uncertain look before stretching.

"How long have you been up?" she asks in her sexy, husky morning voice.

"Few minutes. Had to run the dogs out."

She picks her head up and looks around. "Where are they?"

"Downstairs."

"Sorry. You didn't have to kick them out because of me. I like dogs."

In a sweet gesture that I don't think she gives much thought to, she leans in and kisses my forehead before tossing the covers back. I admire her naked ass all the way to the bathroom and wait for her to come back.

She returns wearing one of my T-shirts.

"I can't vouch for how clean that is if you picked it up off the bathroom floor," I warn her.

Her nose wrinkles and she pulls at the shirt to smell it. "It smells good. Like you."

She jumps on the bed and crawls back under the covers, snuggling up to me.

This is nice.

Real nice. I could totally get used to this.

Maybe it's time to stop fucking around and be straight with her. No more jokes or half-ass attempts. Real shit.

And when she says no, I'll fuck her until she says yes.

Lilly

I hate how much I liked waking up in Z's arms. I like my independence. Sleeping in my own bed. Not having to worry about impressing someone twenty-four seven.

But I really like Z. I'm comfortable around him. Something I never expected.

He's so warm and hard against me, I wriggle, trying to get closer. Not because I'm cold, but because I like how he feels. How *this* feels.

Tipping my head back, I catch him staring at me with an intensity I've never seen. Not sexual.

Something's on Z's mind. On the outside, he seems

calm but I see the pulse in his neck fluttering. I reach over and place my hand over his heart. It's racing.

"What's on your mind, Z? You look like you're about to have a stroke."

He doesn't even crack a smile at my idiotic teasing.

"Last night. Remember how we both admitted we've only been seeing each other?"

"Uh, I don't think that's what we said." He keeps staring at me until I fidget. "We said we hadn't *fucked* anyone else besides each other."

"Same thing," he growls, clearly frustrated with me.

But it's a lie. I've dated a bunch of guys in between seeing Z. I just haven't wanted to *sleep* with a single one. None of them. Try as I might to find someone else, my lady bits were on strike when it came to anyone other than this intense, sexy beast of a man.

"How about we officially only see each other." He doesn't really phrase it as a question. His voice never wavers and his eyes never leave my face, but he's so strained. So serious. And I have the feeling it's killing him not to declare I'm *his*. Like a caveman.

"You want me to be your girlfriend, Z?" I ask, just so I know we're both on the same page.

"I'm a little old for girlfriends, Lilly." He closes his eyes and when he opens them, he's staring somewhere over my shoulder. "But we can start there, if that's easier for you."

Wow. I don't know what else to think. My mind keeps repeating *wowwowowow*. "How does that look? You work in a strip club. You live here. Have girls around just to service you when you're feeling randy. You're on the road a lot. How…?"

The hardening of his expression makes me lose track of my own words.

"You never said anything about Crystal Ball before," he finally says.

"You never wanted to be a couple before."

"Bullshit," he mutters.

"I didn't say *no*. I'm asking questions."

"Fine. You want me to quit my job?"

Shit, do I? It seems unfair. I probably get hit on more often working at the legislature than he does in a strip club.

"No. That's not fair. Either I trust you or I don't."

He turns then, surprise written all over his face. Guess he didn't expect that answer.

"You want me to move out of the clubhouse?"

"Don't you *have* to live here?"

"No. Some of the guys live off-campus," he says with a smirk, as if I'd spoken my frat-house comment out loud last night.

"But you're happy here."

He doesn't say anything. Doesn't have to. I saw with my own eyes last night how at ease he is here. How much he likes being around the guys he considers his family.

"If anyone should move, it's me. You're here. My job's down in Empire…the commute—"

"I come before your job. That's a start," he says dryly.

There's a lot of noise, shouting and banging around, in

the hallway. Nothing alarming. Just the guys waking up and being guys. Z grinds his teeth, as if it's bad timing, but I stop him with a hand on his shoulder.

"In the past, I've had interest from rental agencies…to rent my house out in the summers because it's so close to the lake. I could…I could rent an apartment closer to you." My heart's thumping so hard I barely get the words out.

He flicks his gaze my way and a brief smile touches his lips. "We can talk more about this later."

A breath of relief leaves me. Z's sensitive to my mood. He realizes how hard this is for me and he's giving me space.

"Let's go down for breakfast. I bet the happy couple will be over soon."

"Oh, good. I'd like to see Hope before I leave."

His mouth twists.

"How long do you want me to stick around?"

"I probably shouldn't answer that." He throws the covers off and, in a fluid, sexy motion, pushes himself over top of me, caging me in with his thick, muscled arms. Not even a tremor from holding himself up over me. He dips down and kisses my forehead before moving off the bed.

"You're awfully graceful for such a big guy."

He smirks at me.

"Shit. My bag is down in Trinity's room. I don't have anything to wear besides my bridesmaid dress."

He doesn't tease me or hesitate. "I'll go grab it for you."

Maybe he's good for me after all.

Zero

I got further than I ever expected to with Lilly today. I'm not stupid, though. Sensing it was time to back off, I did. Her mind's turning, working it out in her head. That's enough for now.

Opening the door to run downstairs and grab her stuff, I almost trip over the bags waiting on the floor. I pick them up and turn to Lilly. "Yours?"

She lets out a soft laugh and nods.

Fifteen minutes later, we're headed into the dining room, hand in hand. Trinity's at the usual table, flipping through a big pink binder. "Christ, Trin, the wedding's over. Put that thing away."

Startled, she glances up and slams the binder closed, sliding it under her chair. "Morning."

"Where's your other half?" I ask as we approach the table. Lilly lets me pull a chair out for her and she even sits in it without a single comment.

Trinity points to the doorway, and I turn to see Wrath trying to sneak up on me. "Not today, fucker," I holler, dropping into the chair next to Lilly before he bearhugs me or whatever the fuck else he was planning to do.

He's wearing the same shit-eating grin he had on earlier. "What's up, brother?"

He falls into the chair next to Trinity and flings an arm around her shoulders. "I'll tell you in a few."

Now I'm really curious. But he turns his head,

nuzzling against Trinity's shoulder and whispering something in her ear that makes her laugh.

After a few minutes, she glances around the dining room. "I'll go check on the girls—"

Wrath clamps his hand over her leg, keeping her in place. "Not today," he says, just loud enough for me to hear it.

Lilly catches my eye and I shrug.

Murphy and Teller join us next. Teller looks worn-out while Murphy, I'm not sure what's going on with him. His knuckles on his right hand are scraped up, though. "Get into it last night, little brother?"

For some reason, he and Trinity share a look. "I'll tell you later."

"What the fuck is everyone so secretive for this morning?" I grouch.

Teller bursts out laughing. "Probably waiting for Mom and Dad to get here."

Wrath rolls his eyes. "Christ, they'll both kill you if they hear that."

Lilly shakes against me. "Mom and Dad?"

Murphy makes a circular motion with his hand, indicating everyone at the table. "Rock is the dad—"

"No, no, I get it." Lilly laughs even harder. "No wonder Hope doesn't want kids. She already has a house full of them."

Trinity laughs with her. "Exactly."

Serena and Mariella burst out of the kitchen with

mugs and pour coffee for everyone. Lilly gives me a curious look but doesn't say anything.

"Hey, newlyweds!" Murphy shouts, making all of us turn our heads. Rock sort of glares at each of us and tries to tug Hope back out the door.

"How was the wedding night?" Wrath yells.

I can't resist messing with them either. "Was it worth saving yourself for?" I ask.

Prez rolls his eyes and glances at Hope. "I told you we should have eaten breakfast at home."

She shushes him and they take their seats. Hope's a sharp girl. She looks around the table, taking each of us in. She smiles briefly when she notices Lilly's still here. But her gaze goes back to Wrath and Trinity, who have matching grins stretched across their faces.

"What's up with you two?" she asks.

Right before she says it, I catch Wrath's eye and he looks so fuckin' happy, I know exactly what Trinity's about to say. "We're engaged!"

The girls shriek and Hope races over to see the ring. Lilly joins them and they chatter away. I stand, reaching over to give Wrath a quick hug and back slap. "Congratulations, brother."

I *could* make some ball and chain joke, or get in a dig about how it's about damn time, but I'm too happy for the both of them.

"I am *not* going to any dress shops," Murphy informs all of us. Yeah, that had been fun. For Wrath and me, *not*

Murphy. I eye Wrath because we need to make Murphy do that again, but he's too busy staring at his bride-to-be.

Then they're making out and making everyone want to hurl. Lilly grins at me and leans over to kiss my cheek. "They're sweet together," she whispers.

"He'd do anything for her." I want her to understand, if she let me, I'd be just as devoted to her. I just can't come up with the right words.

Instead, I tease Rock and Hope about all the boring, married sex they'll be having. Teller rats me out for the time or two I said Hope was dick-whipped.

Murphy finally explains why his knuckles are so raw. "I knocked Bull's ass out last night."

I'm sure Bull had that punch coming. Fuck, I wanted to punch him myself last night a few times. Lilly looks a little disgusted, so I shrug. This is who we are. If I want to get serious with her, she might as well hear it all, good and bad.

Serena and Mariella bring out a platter of eggs, bacon, sausage, and toast, which we all demolish.

Wrath informs us he's planning to build a house next. I catch Lilly's eye. *See? I wouldn't expect you to live at the clubhouse,* I want to tell her.

Hope teases us, claiming she got a tattoo that Rock absolutely will not allow her to show us. Lilly leans in. "It must be true love. She always swore she'd *never* get a tattoo."

"Yeah, what about you?"

She raises an eyebrow. "I've never had something I wanted on my body permanently."

"I wanna be on your body permanently," I growl in her ear. She shivers and turns to catch my mouth in a quick kiss.

"For fuck's sake. Y'all need to get a room!" Dex shouts. He's not yelling at me, specifically. Rock and Hope barely glance up at Dex's bitching. Wrath throws his middle finger up without taking his mouth off Trinity.

"Thank fuck," Teller groans, pulling out a chair for Dex. "I'm about to lose my breakfast."

Mariella pokes him in the side, and he grins at her.

Murphy's sitting next to Serena looking like he's choking on a piece of bark. "You okay, lil' brother?"

"I'm good."

"Did Heidi come back last night?" Hope asks Teller who groans.

"No. She called me when he dropped her off, though." He glances over at the bar at the few people snoring on top of it. "Too much going on here last night, you know?"

She laughs. "I see your point."

Rock claps his hands once to get our attention. "Church. Then my bride and I are going to pack for Hawaii."

"Are you *letting* her bring clothes, Rock?" Trinity asks, bursting into giggles.

Rock's mouth twists into a wicked smirk, but he doesn't answer.

"Thanks, Trin," Hope mutters. She's laughing too, though.

Rock glances at me but before he says anything, Murphy stands. "I'm gonna walk Serena out and then I'll round the guys up for church."

I think it's news to Serena that she's leaving.

"Thanks for all your help, Serena," Mariella calls out.

Serena nods and follows Murphy.

After they clear the dining room, Trinity jumps up. "While you guys are in church, I *am* helping Mariella clean up," she says with a pointed look at Wrath, who rolls his eyes. Hope joins her before Rock can say no.

"I feel like I should help now too," Lilly jokes.

I lean into her. "We won't be long. Will you still be here?"

She turns and presses a quick kiss to my lips. Her fingers trail over my cheek and she looks into my eyes. "I'll stick around."

EPILOGUE

A FEW WEEKS LATER...

Zero

"How do you feel about taking a vote on Axel today?" Rock asks Wrath and me.

We're in the office getting ready to sit down for church with all the brothers in a few minutes.

"Seriously?" Wrath asks. "Why now?"

Rock tilts his head and stares at both of us. "Really? You need me to say it?"

Poor Murphy. The bastard's so hung up on Heidi, there is no fuckin' way he's voting her boyfriend into the club. Best we quit wasting Axel's time now. As nice as the kid can be, he's always seemed off. The club's something for him to *do*, not who he is or wants to be. I don't trust him one-hundred percent. Not that I haven't felt that way about a brother once or twice in the past before they patched-in but this seems different.

"We all know how it's gonna go down," I say. "Rip it off now like a Band-Aid."

"Speaking of pathetic bastards," Wrath says, looking at me. "Where ya been lately?"

I don't feel like admitting that I haven't seen or heard from Lilly in weeks. Here I thought we'd finally worked things out and were in an actual relationship. *Surprise!* We're not. Am I gonna discuss it with Wrath? Nope.

I run my hand over the back of my neck and look away. "Taking care of things."

"What things?"

"Leave him alone." Rock punches Wrath's shoulder. Not that it will stop Wrath. He runs his shrewd gaze over me for a second before leaving the office. As I try to follow him, Rock stops me.

"Everything all right?"

"Yeah."

"Your brother?"

I shrug. He's asking about one of my dipwad bio-brothers. "Checked him into a new place. Doubt it'll do much good."

The look Rock gives me is sympathetic but not pitying. "If you need anything, let me know."

"Thanks, brother."

Church ends up being an epic fucking disaster. Teller almost kills Axel, then mouths off to Rock. By the end of the whole fiasco, I'm done.

Out.

And I know just where I'm going.

She can dodge my phone calls. Ignore my texts. But showing up on her damn doorstep has worked before and it'll work again.

I'm not giving up this woman without a fight.

The ride up to Lake George clears my mind. It's a crisp, cold fall afternoon. Perfect riding weather. The leaves have all changed to blazing shades of red and gold but haven't dropped yet. My favorite part of living in upstate New York.

I'm contemplating whether to break into her house if she's not home. Maybe surprise her by making dinner or something corny like that.

The unfamiliar sedan parked out front? I didn't expect her to have someone over.

Some dude she's seeing? Her family? Maybe she got a new car?

Only one way to find out.

I pull right up to the house so there's no way whoever is inside can't hear me coming. If Lilly's as smart as I know she is, she'll realize it's me and come outside.

But it's not Lilly who greets me when I get off my bike.

It's a fucking shotgun.

"Whoa." I hold up my hands and back up a few steps from the maniac on the porch. "Easy, man."

"Who the fuck are you?" the old man shouts. "And what are you doing here?"

A woman comes out behind him, also carrying a

shotgun. I glance around. Did I accidentally show up at the wrong fucking house?

Remembering Lilly's story about the shotgun her brother insisted she keep in the house, I wonder if these are relatives of hers.

"I'm a friend of Lilly's. Just stopped by to see her."

The man lowers his shotgun. The woman doesn't. Smart lady.

"There's no Lilly here," the woman says. "Just us."

"That's the woman who owns the home," the guy says to his wife.

"Oh." She sets her shotgun down. "Sorry. You're the first person who's shown up here unannounced."

"Yeah, sorry about that. So, is Lilly here?"

"We're renting the house from her."

Wait, what? We talked about her renting out her house. So she could come live near *me*. But since she's not living with me and I haven't heard from her, I'm not sure what to do with this information.

"Since when?"

The couple stares at each other. "Since the first of the month? House wasn't listed for rent long."

"You talk to her?"

"No, we go through a rental company. Talked to her brother about some issues we had though."

Fucking Alex. I'll be dammed if I'm going to track that asshole down and beg him for information about his sister.

"We have a number for her," the woman says.

"That's all right." I have her damn cell phone. She never answers it. "I have her cell."

"No, it's a work number, I think. Hang on." The woman steps inside and returns a few seconds later and hands me a piece of pink paper with a phone number scrawled across the top. 8-1-8 area code.

"Thanks." I tuck the paper in my pocket. "Sorry to bother you."

I wait until I get down the road before pulling into a gas station parking lot. I shut down my bike and take out my phone and the number.

Am I really going to just call her when she obviously skipped town?

What the fuck? We said we would try this relationship thing, and she disappeared on me instead. My pride doesn't feel like dialing her new number.

"Fuck it." I Google the number first. It's some generic-sounding health sciences company. In California.

California?

This has to be a joke.

A chipper receptionist answers on the first ring. Not Lilly. I clear my throat before asking to speak with her.

"Oh, she's not in today. Can I take a message?"

"No, thanks." Before hanging up, I confirm the address of the place and that Lilly works there.

Am I really considering taking a cross-country trip?

The more important question?

What the fuck's she doing in California?

**Zero Tolerance (Lost Kings MC #12)
is now available!**

As Vice President of the Lost Kings Motorcycle Club, I've spent a lot of years as a hit-it-and-quit-it player only seeking a good time. Willing women are never in short supply.

I never needed any of them for more than one night.

Until I met her.

My perfect woman. Like a damn mermaid, she was beautiful, smart, sexy, and slippery as fuck.

I thought I'd convinced her we'd be good together long-term, but then she disappeared without a word.

Two years.

That's how long it's been since I saw her.

Just as I finally moved on, my mythical woman resurfaces.

She forgot to mention one little thing before she vanished.

One small secret growing up into a big lie.

It's a betrayal too deep to overcome.

I should hate her.

Even though she's heartbreak wrapped in a seductive package.

I want her more than ever.

Autumn prefers her romances on the classier side of dirty. Romances with loving alpha heroes are her favorite-the bigger the better.

Her past lives include baking cookies, bagging groceries, selling cheap shoes, and practicing law. Playing with her imaginary friends all day is by far her favorite job yet!

Autumn lives in upstate New York with her own alpha hero.

Sign up for her newsletter to be notified of releases, sales, events, and special sneak peeks at future projects!

www.autumnjoneslake.com

The End

www.ingramcontent.com/pod-product-compliance
Lightning Source LLC
Chambersburg PA
CBHW070459170726
48291CB00008B/2575